Gooflumps

STAY OUT OF THE BATHROOM

R. U. SLIME

An Unauthorized Parody

Not a Goosebumps Book

Bullseye Books

Random House 🏠 New York

An Unauthorized Parody

Not a Goosebumps Book

A BULLSEYE BOOK PUBLISHED BY RANDOM HOUSE, INC.

Copyright © 1995 by Robert Hughes. All rights reserved under
International and Pan-American Copyright Conventions.
Published in the United States by Random House, Inc., New York,
and simultaneously in Canada by Random House of Canada
Limited, Toronto.

Library of Congress Catalog Card Number: 95-070043
ISBN: 0-679-87908-0
RL: 4.01

Manufactured in the United States of America
10 9 8 7 6 5

CHAPTER 1

"You are totally dead, man!" Roger cried.

He had chased me three levels up from Command Control with a full commando force at his back. His Venusian mercenaries were armed to the teeth with photon rifles.

I was all by myself—cornered, outnumbered—just the way I like it. "You'll never get me!" I yelled back at him.

"I totally control your whole flagship, man!" Roger said. "You are all alone! You can't fight anymore! Give it up, man!"

"No way!" I screamed, retreating down the corridor.

I had no idea if my plan was working or not. The Venusian mercenaries were following me, though. That was a good sign. I ran through the maze of dimly lit corridors. I kept expecting to see a squadron of Martians come around the corner and cut me off at any minute.

Up another level—almost there! The Venusians were right on my heels!

I slammed into the ladder that led to the Secret Emergency Control Room at full speed. I put my foot on the first rung and a photon bolt nearly blew it off.

I swung around and brought my Kolodner 800 energy rifle up at the same time.

It was a Centauran—and it had me in its sights!

"Eat fire, slimebrain!" I roared. I pulled the trigger and the barrel flashed with pure firepower.

I flew up the ladder. Roger was coming up right behind me—just where I wanted him. Another bolt hit the wall beside me as I spun the lock on the hatchway.

"Give up, dude!" Roger yelled. "Hey, what are you doing?"

"Come on up and find out!" I yelled down at him, punching the combination on the control panel.

The door swung open and I stepped inside the Secret Emergency Control Room. Just across the small room—there it was!

Roger came in behind me and stopped.

"What is this place?" he asked, covering me with his photon rifle. "I didn't see this in your layout."

"That's 'cause it's not on my layout, pinhead!" I spotted the flashing button across the room.

Then Roger saw it and his eyes went wide. "No way, you can't do that!"

I saw my chance and I took it. My foot went up, and with one kick I sent his photon rifle skidding across the floor. Then I went and locked the door from the inside.

"No way, dude!" he complained.

"Yes way, dude!" I told him. I stepped over to the button.

"You can't do that, man. You'll blow your whole ship up!"

"I know—with your whole army on it!" I shot back.

"But that's against the Rules of Intergalactic Warfare!" he said.

"I know!" I said, laughing. I hit the button. I'm crazy like that. Ask anybody.

"I win!" I screamed as my flagship began to rumble. Then it blew apart into a thousand flaming shards of annihilation!

Roger threw down his joystick and glared at me.

I pointed at the computer monitor. "Pretty cool, huh?" I asked, grinning. Meanwhile, the Armies of Evil game was computing our statistics and figuring the body counts.

I love body counts.

"That's totally not in the rules!" Roger whined. Roger Douglas is my best friend, even if he is the Dork of the Universe. He's also really smart—and that counts for something, I guess.

"Check subsection seventeen, under 'Secret Self-Destruct Option,'" I told him.

He smiled and took a bite of his bologna sandwich. "Anyway, it's a tie, because I totally destroyed your army too. Man, this bread is stale."

"Check the stats," I told him. "Especially look at your homeworld population."

Roger looked at me and then punched in the command for Homeworld Information. Suddenly he gasped.

"That's right—ten thousand more than last time you checked. I transported almost my whole army off the ship onto your homeworld before you ever boarded me, dude! DorkWorld is at my mercy!"

"It's not DorkWorld, geekbrain!" he cried. "It's RogerWorld!"

"Same thing!" I told him, taking a bite of my own sandwich.

"Too bad the atmosphere of RogerWorld is poisonous to your guys," Roger said.

"What?" I cried. I punched up the information. It was true! My whole army had about two hours left to live!

"Ha, ha, ha! It's a tie, dude!" Roger cried.

I jumped across the couch at him and got him in a headlock, yelling, "The Noogie Master strikes again!" He tried to get away as I dug my knuckle into his head.

"Ow, ow!" he cried. "Hey, cut it out!"

"Say 'You're the king of Armies of Evil,'" I told him.

"Never!" he shouted. We both hit the floor and rolled across the carpet. There wasn't anybody around to tell us to stop fighting—the ideal conditions to invite someone over, in my opinion.

My dad was out in the backyard doing yard work. He was on a two-week vacation from his engineering company—and all he'd been doing for the first week was yard work.

My mom was still at the office. She's a

part-time paralegal at a law firm downtown. She used to be a secretary, but then she recently went back to law school. She's going to be a lawyer in a couple of years. Which means she works and studies constantly.

There was no one to stop me. I was going to give Roger the noogie of the century.

Crash!

"Oh, dude!" Roger cried.

It was my glass of milk. I'd knocked it over with my foot, and now it was all over the floor.

"Thanks a lot, geeko!" I said.

"I didn't do anything, pinhead!" Roger shot back.

"You made me give you noogies," I told him. "If you hadn't done that I wouldn't have spilled the milk!"

"Oh, that makes a lot of sense," he said.

"Makes about as much sense as me beating you up for it!" I threatened him. I would never do it, but—you know. You have to at least say these things.

"Oh, like you're going to beat Lumpy Leudke's face in?"

I had to fight Lumpy after school on Monday. He was a big guy. I wasn't scared or anything.

"Yeah, maybe I'll practice on you!" I snarled at him.

Roger puffed his chest out and crossed his arms. "Yeah? Just try it!" he warned me.

We stared at each other, making our meanest faces. We circled around..

I shot my hand out. "Thumb wrestle!"

Roger locked fingers with me. "To the death," he growled through his teeth.

"To the death," I agreed, nodding my head.

We counted down together. "Three, two, one! Go!"

But just before we started, there was a sick, horrible wailing sound.

"Help me! Please! Help!" somebody shrieked.

Roger looked at me. "Did you hear that?" he asked. "It sounded like an alien!"

"Yeah, I think it was my sister," I told him. My sister, the neat freak monster.

"Somebody, please come save me!" she shrieked again. It was my sister. And the screams were coming from the upstairs bathroom!

"Look out, Roger! I'm going in!" I yelled, dashing up the stairs.

I kicked open the door.

Cynthia was leaning back against the sink, spraying the toilet with Darling Debbie Disinfectant Spray.

"Whoa!" Roger gasped, looking around at the bathroom. It was a mess. There was water all over the floor and wet toilet-paper balls clinging to the walls.

"Looks good, huh?" I asked him.

"You are such a little monster!" Cynthia yelled at me. "I can't believe you left the bathroom like this. You didn't even put the seat down!" she raged. She aimed the disinfectant at me and sprayed.

I dodged out of the way. "Hey, you could blind somebody with that!" I told her. "Not that she needs that spray stuff to blind anybody," I whispered to Roger.

"Aw, c'mon Joe," he whispered back. He won't ever admit it, but he kind of has a crush on Cynthia.

Which is scarier than a messy bathroom any day. Actually, it's even scarier than the smell of Darling Debbie Disinfectant Spray, and that's bad.

"I can't believe you, Joe! How could you make this mess and then not clean it up?"she demanded. "How many times has Mom told you to put the seat down?"

"Well, sis, the way I see it, why should I put the seat down for you when you won't even consider putting it back up for me? I mean, isn't that what equal rights are all about?" I turned to Roger. "Same old story. They want to be treated the same as guys and you still have to hold the door open for them!"

"Like you've ever held the door open for anybody," Roger commented. "Remember the time you slammed it on Jackie Jones?"

I laughed. "That was awesome, wasn't it?" Jackie hadn't spoken to me since, which was the best thing of all.

Cynthia's hands were balled up into fists. Her perfectly painted Darling Debbie Daring Dewberry fingernails dug into her palms. Her eyes were practically popping out of her head. "I hate you, Joe! Why don't you die! Die! Die!"

Don't let Cynthia fool you. We're really close.

Yeah. Right.

"I have to get ready for cheerleader practice and this place is a disaster area!" she screeched.

"Why don't you use the other bathroom?" I suggested.

"You know very well why I don't use it!" she screamed.

"Why, 'cause it's in the basement?" I asked.

"No!"

"And the basement is scary?"

"No!"

"And you're scared to go down there without somebody holding your itsy-bitsy hand?"

That was too much for her.

"That's it, you're going to get it so bad when I tell Mom and Dad about this!" She stormed out of the bathroom.

"Oh, man, Joe, that was great! You really let her have it!" Crush or no crush, Roger appreciated the work of a master. He started applauding my performance.

I jumped up on the toilet and took a big bow.

"It was nothing. No, really. Any genius could have bugged Cynthia that bad!" I said.

"Did you really mess up the bathroom just to peeve her?" he asked me.

"Mostly," I told him. "And also because I just like messing things up. Especially in here!"

Roger nodded. "It's a pretty ugly bath-room," he agreed, looking around. The bath-room is all puke pink and grotty green. "It almost looks better trashed."

"Yeah, but I put the finishing touches on it, Rog. And you wanna know why?" I asked. I cupped my hands over my mouth and started swaying back and forth, making rap noises.

Roger grinned. "No, why's that, homey?"

"Well, I'll tell you," I said. And I started rapping:

"I'm the bathroom master
I'm a real bowl blaster
Don't mess with me
'Cause I can mess it up faster
With just one flush
I can make a toilet gush
When my sister cleans it up
I just turn her to mush!"

I was dancing around pretty wildly. Then suddenly, the whole toilet lurched over onto its side.

Crack! I slid across the floor and crashed into the tub.

"Dude!" I cried. "What—what happened?"

CHAPTER
2

The damage was even worse than I thought. Not only was the toilet upended, but the bowl was cracked.

Water started flowing out of the broken toilet bowl, spreading all over the floor. Flood emergency!

"You have a serious plumbing problem, Joe!" Roger announced.

What a genius. I told you he was smart.

Plus, his father's a plumber, so Roger thinks he's an expert.

Water splashed up over my legs. I was getting soaked! "Do something," I told Roger as I hauled myself up. "Fast!"

Roger bent over and looked at the toilet. Even though he does act like a know-it-all, it's pretty cool that he knows all about toilets and pipes and junk.

"It looks like you cracked the toilet bowl," Roger said.

"Duh," I said.

The water was headed for the bathroom door. I grabbed a towel and started sopping it up. It was one of our "good" towels, but this was an emergency.

"Can we fix it?" I demanded. I wiped the towel over the tiles on the floor. But the water kept on coming! "Seek higher ground!" I yelled. "Roger! What are we going to do?"

"Chill. My dad has some waterproof tape in his toolbox. We could try that," Roger said, scratching his head.

"Well, go get it!" I cried.

"First, you have to say something," he said with an evil smile.

The water was still pouring out. I got another towel and threw it on the floor. It made a wet slapping sound as it hit the tiles. "What do I have to say, geekbrain?"

"Who's the king of Armies of Evil?" he asked.

"I am," I told him. "Now go get the tape!"

"Who's the king?" he asked again. He smiled even more and swished a big puddle of water around with the toe of his Converse sneaker.

"If I say it, will you go get the stupid tape?" I asked.

"Sure I will," he teased.

I am the king of Armies of Evil—everybody knows that! But I also knew that if the water started pouring down the hall, I would be in big trouble on planet Mom!

"Okay, okay—you're the king of Armies of Evil. You're the greatest general the whole galaxy has ever seen! Will you get the tape now!"

Roger nodded, grinning happily. "And you have to tell everybody in school that, too!"

"Yeah, right," I muttered under my breath. All the towels were soaked. And the water was still coming! I guess all that junk about being super-absorbent is just a lie.

Roger splashed through the water to the door. "Okay, I'll be right back," he said. He jerked the door open, slipped through, and slammed it closed behind him.

King of Armies of Evil—that's a laugh!

I put down the last towel right after Roger left. Then I started unrolling the toilet paper and putting that all over the floor. Pretty soon, I was covered with bits of wet peach-colored toilet paper. When I peeled it off my hands and arms, it looked like big pieces of skin coming off. I wet some and put it on my face and looked in the mirror.

I looked like a mummy!

I stuck my arms straight out and made a scary face. "Rraahhh! You have disturbed the mummy's tomb, now you must suffer the mummy's curse!" I growled.

Knock! Knock! Knock!

Oh, no! Someone was at the door! If they opened it, the water would soak them in the hallway!

"Joe, what are you doing in there?" Cynthia demanded. "Did you clean up yet?"

I had to think fast! If Miss Neat came in and saw this mess, I'd be grounded for life, stuck cleaning the bathroom with a package of Darling Debbie Drybaby Diaper Dropcloths!

Try saying that three times fast.

"Cynthia, don't come in! I'm...I'm sick!" I lied.

"What's the matter with you? You weren't sick before! Except sick in the head, but that's, like, an ongoing condition."

I moaned. I groaned. I gagged. All the usual noises I make when I go to the school nurse. Wasn't anything working? Was my sister completely heartless?

"I don't know—it must've been the old bologna!" I gasped.

The bologna Roger and I had eaten for lunch had been past the freshness date. I'd dared him to eat it, because I can eat almost anything and never get sick. It's a little game I made up a few years ago called Expiration Date. That talent comes in handy because my mom and dad don't always have time to shop for groceries. I'm still alive, but a container of spoiled ricotta cheese almost killed me last year.

"I told you not to eat that bologna!" Cynthia said nastily.

How did I know she was going to say that?

I made another gagging noise.

"You want me to get you something?" she asked. Now she actually sounded kind of concerned. Cynthia could be all right when she wanted to be.

Which was about a week out of the year.

"No, that's okay. I'll be all right—Roger went to get some medicine from his house," I croaked.

"You sure you don't want me to come in?" she asked.

"*Bllaaahhh—blllecchh,*" I improvised. I'm

16

pretty good at faking if I do say so myself. *"Blllllaaaabb!* No, don't come in! It's really gross in here. I'll be all right in a minute. Thanks, though."

She didn't say anything for a minute. "Okay, I have to go to cheerleading practice anyway," she said finally. "I'm late already. Feel better!" I could hear her taking the stairs two at a time.

"Where *are* you, Roger?" I muttered between clenched teeth.

I took the toothbrush holder, put the brushes on the counter, and started bailing water into the sink.

Why didn't I think of that before?

Then I found a whole unopened pack of these square things under the sink. They were all different colors. I had no idea what they were. But I figured anything would help at this point.

I opened the package and threw them all over the floor. Before I knew what was happening, they started expanding and growing—bigger and bigger, as if they were alive! They looked like giant sea creatures— *"Aaabbb!"* I screamed.

Roger opened the door. "How come you're yelling at the sponges?"

"Oh, those are *sponges*," I sighed. Phew. What a relief. "I always wondered what those looked like."

"I saw Cynthia on my way up and she said you were spewing. Are you really sick?" he asked.

"Yeah, I'm really sick—of your face!" I said. "Where's the stupid tape?"

Roger frowned and handed over the tape. "Man, what a grump!"

"Well, it looks like it's holding," I said, looking around the bathroom about ten minutes later.

"Yeah, and you can barely see it," Roger agreed. The crack in the toilet was near the back, and the tape was white. So if you weren't looking for it, you could hardly tell it was there.

Roger had cleaned up the bathroom while I put the tape on. It was all spick-and-span now. I had replaced the wet towels with new ones. I even got more toilet paper. I felt like the school janitor, Bob, who I "accidentally" kicked over once while he was cleaning the floor. I told the stupid principal I was practicing my karate and Bob just happened to get in the way. It could happen.

I held up my hand and Roger high-fived me. "Thanks, man," I said. I meant it, too. I can be really deep and emotional when I want to. I can feel your pain.

Usually because I'm the one who caused it.

"Oh, you're all choked up. What are you going to do now? Cry?" Roger said sarcastically.

"No. Hey, you want a donut for helping me?" I asked him.

"Yeah, what kind do you have?" he asked.

I punched him in the arm as hard as I could.

"Ow," he complained, rubbing his arm.

"We have a dozen Hurts Donuts. I can't believe you fell for that one, man! Hurts, don' it?" I was doubled up from laughing.

"What are you boys doing in here?" my dad's voice boomed out suddenly.

I looked up. He was standing in the doorway smiling at us. He had on the jeans he wears for yard work. He was covered with dirt and smelled kind of bad. Like most of the dads in our neighborhood.

"Uh, nothing, Dad! I was just cleaning up the bathroom and Roger was helping me," I said.

"Are you sick or something?" Dad put his hand on my forehead, as if he was taking my temperature.

"No. I just thought it was time I started doing more around the house," I told him with a big smile.

"Uh-huh, right." He nodded. "Well, whatever you did it for—thanks. I think. Now you two clear out of here. I want to wash all this dirt off me before your mom gets home," he said, stepping into the bathroom.

"Okay, Dad, see you later," I said as the door closed.

"Good-bye, Mr. Kohler," Roger said.

The door shut. *Click.* It was locked.

Roger and I stood in the hall for a minute. My dad was humming some old song from his hippie days. We heard the water in the shower go on.

"No problem," I said to Roger. "The coast is clear!"

Then it happened—the big flush!

There was a loud crash! Water started flowing out from under the door. The hallway carpet was doing a great job of soaking it up.

"Joseph!" my father yelled.

Uh-oh.

CHAPTER 3

"Looks like you're going to need a new unit, John," Roger's father said, tapping the toilet lightly with his wrench.

"You can't fix it?" Dad asked.

Mr. Douglas shook his head. "I would if I could, but your bowl's cracked." He shook his head again as he got up from the bathroom floor.

It was more than cracked! The toilet was tilting at a weird angle, even though we'd put it back in an upright position. It was finished—and so was I!

"Joe, get in here!" Dad called.

I was standing in the hall with my mother. She looked at me in a disappointed way, then she kind of shoved me into the bathroom.

"Joseph, tell us the truth," Dad said. "What exactly happened here?"

"I—I—I was dancing on it," I said quietly.

"You were *what*?" he asked.

"Just a little," I defended myself.

Mr. Douglas laughed. "You must have been doing a Virginia reel to damage a sturdy old sanitary unit like that!"

"A sanitary unit?" I asked. Never mind what a Virginia reel was. Now I knew where Roger's geek gene came from!

"That's what we call them in the plumbing business. It doesn't sound as bad as saying toilet all the time," Roger's dad explained.

Mom stepped into the bathroom. She still had her work clothes on. "Well, whatever you call it—how much does a new one cost?"

"That depends on what you're looking for," Mr. Douglas said. He threw his wrench in the toolbox on the counter and scratched his bald head.

I couldn't wait until Roger went bald. I was going to make so much fun of him, he'd have to get a fake hairpiece, then I could make fun of that.

But I'm getting carried away. We're only twelve. Roger has at least ten years left before he turns into Mr. Clean.

"There's a new one just came out, really nice, quiet as a whisper, and water-economical, too. It's called the Ultra Flush 2000," Mr. Douglas explained.

"How much is it?" Dad asked. "Sounds expensive."

"That one'll run you about three hundred," Mr. Douglas said.

Mom gasped. Money was kind of tight, with her going back to school and all.

"Three hundred dollars—that's pretty steep!" Dad said.

"But that's the top of the line. You can get them for a lot less," Mr. Douglas told him.

"Well, that's good," Dad sighed. He turned to me. "Do you know how long it would take you to pay that off out of your allowance?" he asked me.

"About a bizillion years," I said.

Dad looked me right in the eye. "At least."

Mr. Douglas closed his toolbox and picked it up. "You sure Roger didn't have anything to do with this?" he asked me.

I shook my head. No use both of us being in trouble.

"Okay," he said. He messed up my hair.

I hate when people do that. It's like, get

your hand off my head, I'm not a cat.

"Don't be too hard on him, John," he said to my dad as he clumped down the stairs in his big boots. "It was a pretty old sanitary unit, after all."

I looked up at Dad hopefully. He frowned at me and then tweaked my ear a little. He saw somebody do that on an old black-and-white TV show once and he thinks it's what dads are supposed to do all the time. I figure, he'll grow out of it by the time I'm taller than him—or else.

"So, what do we do now?" Mom asked.

"I guess we have dinner. Tomorrow we'll go out and get a new one," Dad said.

"Will there be anyplace open on Sunday?" Mom asked.

Dad shrugged. "We'll find one...won't we, son?" He grinned at me.

Me? Shop for toilets—on a Sunday, my day off? I already had the whole day planned. Sleep until noon, go for a lazy bike ride, eat a huge bag of cheese curls...

Two thousand plans...down the drain.

"I probably shouldn't go, Dad. I'd just be in the way!" I protested. That was what they always told me when I wanted to go places I shouldn't go.

"Nonsense. You knew enough about them to break one—"

"But, Dad—"

"Joe, either you come with me tomorrow and help me get a new one—or you pay for it out of your allowance for the next bizillion years!" he announced sternly.

"But...I was going to go bike riding tomorrow, Dad," I said. "Really far!" Parents love it when you exercise, for some weird reason.

"What about me? I'm on vacation—you think I want to go shopping for a new sanitary unit?"

"No, I guess not," I had to admit.

"Okay, then, it's settled!" he said.

"Gleepnorp's Sanitary Units and Appliances? What's a Gleepnorp?" I asked.

We'd been driving around for two hours looking for a place to buy a toilet. It was Sunday, so everything was closed. We'd tried to go to Bob's Appliances in town, but there was a sign in the window saying that they were closed for an emergency.

Maybe their toilet broke, too. Maybe it was an epidemic!

Finally, we headed down I-97 and drove

through Floville, where my Aunt Thelma lives.

"I don't know, Joe. Maybe Gleepnorp is a Russian brand name. The place looks open, though."

It could've been Russian. We were learning in school all about how Russia was broken up into all these little countries now. And they did have funny names over there. They probably thought our names were pretty funny, too.

If you say your name over and over again, you have to admit it does start to sound pretty weird. Kohler. Koh...ler. Kol—her. After a while you can even start spelling it wrong.

Okay, so back to the Great American Sanitary-Unit Search, as I was calling it. G.A.S.S. for short.

"It looks like they have a sale going on," Dad said, pointing to a sign in the dirty window. The sign said:

BIG SALE!
ONE DAY ONLY!

It did look open and it did look like they were having a sale. But it also looked kind of creepy, as if they needed a major sale to get anyone to go inside!

"Well, should we go in and take a look? It can't hurt," Dad said.

I was still drinking a root beer I'd gotten at the Weenieporium. "I just want to finish my soda. I'll be right in." There was a sign in the window that said NO FOOD OR DINKS ALLOWED.

Someone had rubbed the "R" in "Drinks" off. Good thing Roger hadn't come along.

Why did they care whether people ate or drank inside the place, anyway. It was a toilet store—as if it would matter!

"Okay, buddy, see you inside," Dad said. He stepped up to the door. I felt a whoosh of really cold air as Dad went in, as if he was walking into a refrigerator.

Then I could barely see him. The windows were grimy and it was dark inside.

I'd say it was a weird sanitary-unit store, but then again, I've never been to any others. I had nothing to compare it with. And I didn't plan on comparison shopping any time soon, either.

I was standing there blowing bubbles in my root beer, fantasizing about riding bikes and swimming in the reservoir, when I heard a giant crash from behind the store.

I tiptoed around the side of the store.

Then I heard another crash.

I peeked around the corner. All I could see at first was a bunch of trash cans and a wrecked car.

Or was it really wrecked?

I'd never seen a car like this before. It was like a huge custom minivan. It was white, two stories tall, and had a flashing light on the roof. The body was more round than square, and it was higher in the back than in the front. It looked like a small squished starship *Enterprise*.

Wait a second! What if it was an alien spaceship?

"What are you doing back here?" a voice yelled. A green furry figure started rising out of the trash can closest to me.

"O—O—Oscar?" I stammered.

CHAPTER
4

"Get out of here, Joe-Joe!"

"Aunt Thelma?" I cried. What was Aunt Thelma doing here? Okay, so she lives in Floville, and she has the right to go shopping, but this was ridiculous!

"Hiya, Joe-Joe!" she said, heaving her bulk out of the trash can. She's the only person in the world who still calls me Joe-Joe. That was my nickname when I was a baby. I hate it! If anybody else calls me Joe-Joe, though...watch out!

I ran over to her as she was brushing herself off. She was wearing a green fur-trimmed pantsuit that was in style in the fifties. It *belonged* in the garbage. It didn't really fit right, either. But that figures. Aunt Thelma gets all her clothes at garage sales.

"What are you doing in that trash can, Aunt Thelma?"

She grabbed my face and gave me a big kiss. "Oh, anything for a thrill!"

"Where's your bike?" I asked her. She only rides bikes. She says that cars are a curse because they pollute and stuff.

As if bikes aren't a curse. Have you ever gotten a flat tire? Tried to lasso someone with the chain and gotten grease all over your shirt?

"My bike's right over there behind the trash can," she told me. "Now, what are you doing here?"

"We have to get a new toilet. Dad's inside buying one now," I explained. "Why did you yell at me to get away from that old car?" I asked, pointing at the wreck of a machine. "Or whatever it is! It looks like a grounded spaceship. Like from the early days of the space program, before they figured out the basics! Did you buy that at a garage sale, too?"

"You say your dad's inside the store right now?" she asked, ignoring my question.

I nodded.

"Well, let's go in and say hello," she said. She grabbed my hand. We walked around to the front of the store and went in.

"Hello, Thelma. What are you doing here?" Dad asked, looking up from a toilet.

Aunt Thelma and my dad don't get along very well. Dad says it's because he's a scientist and she's a wacko. She believes in spirits and flying saucers and Dad says all of that is bunk, whatever that means. He never calls her a wacko in front of Mom, though. He can be really considerate, like me.

"Oh, I was just passing by and I saw Joe-Joe out front," she lied.

"But, Aunt Thelma, you were—" I began.

Aunt Thelma kicked me with her heel. I guessed that meant to shut up, so I did.

Dad nodded and went back to looking at toilets. I don't know what the big decision was—there seemed to be only one kind in the whole store.

And the store was even creepier than it had looked from the outside. It was totally freezing inside and the lights were very dim. There were just rows and rows of this one kind of toilet lined up across the floor...in formation, like an army, as far as the eye could see.

Then one of the toilets started moving toward us!

CHAPTER
5

It wasn't a toilet. It was a salesman wearing a white suit.

He walked up to my dad. He acted as if he didn't even see Aunt Thelma and me. He leaned down close to my dad and said, "Have you made a selection yet, sir?"

He was one weird-looking dude! His skin was sort of greenish, but his voice was the strangest thing about him. It was kind of like he was whispering and wheezing and gargling at the same time.

Aunt Thelma stepped forward. "John, I'd suggest that you buy your toilet elsewhere."

The salesman's head snapped around and he stared at Aunt Thelma. He moved really weird—kind of jerky-like. Like his head and arms were attached by rubber bands.

Dad winced and looked at Aunt Thelma. "Oh, and why's that, Thelma? Are all the toilets here haunted or something?" he asked sarcastically. "Do they have bad karma?"

The salesman, who was still staring at Aunt Thelma, said, "I assure you, madame, we have the best prices in the universe. Uh...town, I mean!"

"I'm sure you do," Aunt Thelma retorted. "But just what kind of a name is Gleepnorp, anyway?"

"Thelma, I'm surprised at you!" Dad interrupted. "You're always so open-minded. What do you care where he's from?"

The salesman's head snapped back toward my dad. "That is quite all right, sir," he wheezed. "It is true that I am not from near here. I come from a place far, far away. A beautiful place—very different from Floville. I come from a place called Polaris!"

We all gasped. "Polaris is the North Star!" I cried.

The salesman winced. He jerked his head around and looked at me—creep city!

"Polaris, New Jersey," he quickly said. "It is...how you say...a sister city to one in Belarus. Many of us have come to America from there."

Belarus is one of those little countries that used to be Russia. Dad was right.

Aunt Thelma still didn't seem convinced.

"Well, wherever he's from, John, I still don't think that—"

Dad cut her off. "Thelma, we need a toilet. This guy is going to give me a great price. And besides, nowhere else is open."

"Can't you wait until tomorrow—just one day?" she pleaded.

Didn't Aunt Thelma ever have to go to the bathroom? I wondered. Or was she even weirder than I thought? I didn't like this Gleepnorp dude, either, but a toilet's a toilet.

"Why should I wait? I can get one right now and Tim Douglas can install it tonight," he told her, turning to the salesman. "Now how much did you say that was?"

"Just come with me, sir, and I'll write you out a bill," he said in his weird voice.

Dad walked over to the counter. I turned around to say something to Aunt Thelma, but the front door was just swinging shut.

I ran outside, hoping to catch her. But all I could see was a speck of green on the horizon. Aunt Thelma was gone! Man, could she ride that three-speed fast or what?

*   *   *

34

"Well, that should just about do it," Mr. Douglas announced. He replaced the little cover on the back of the unit, and stood up.

"Thanks for coming over, Tim," Dad said.

"Don't thank me until you get my bill!" Mr. Douglas joked.

We were all crowded into the bathroom— me and Roger and Mr. Douglas and Cynthia and Mom and Dad. We stared at the new toilet as if it was a new baby about to utter its first word.

The tank gurgled.

"Ooh, it's beautiful," Cynthia cooed. "And so clean!"

"Well, now that this whole toilet thing is behind us," I said, clasping my hands together, "how about an Armies of Evil rematch, Rog?"

"Sounds good to me," Roger agreed.

As soon as we started out of the bathroom, Dad put his hand on my shoulder. "Just a minute there, big boy. We have a family meeting planned for right now."

A family meeting? I'd rather go back to the toilet store. I'd rather *be* a toilet.

"Into the family room now, Joe," Mom said. "March!"

I was trapped like a rat.

I grabbed Roger's hand and shook it firmly. "I'll call you tonight. If you don't hear from me by ten o'clock—call out the National Guard!"

"Sure thing, buddy. It was nice knowing you," Roger said. He and his dad left, and we all went downstairs and sat in the family room. Except Cynthia. She was out in the kitchen getting something to drink.

"We're sorry to have to do this, Joe, but until you learn to clean up after yourself and not treat toilets like toys, things are going to have to change," Dad said.

"What's going to change?" Cynthia asked. "Did I miss something?" She came back into the family room with a big glass of diet cola.

"From now on, your mother and I will have the upstairs bathroom, and you kids will share the downstairs bathroom," Dad announced.

Cynthia was in the middle of taking a huge swallow of soda. Her eyes went wide and she spit the soda out onto the rug.

Mom turned to Dad in a panic. "I think she's choking!" she cried.

Cynthia wasn't choking—even I could tell that. She was hurling—cool!

"Please, please, please, oh, please don't

make me share a bathroom with Joe!"

Mom put her hands on her hips. "Is *that* what this is all about?"

Cynthia ran over to Dad. "Please don't make me share a bathroom with The Pest! I'll do anything. I'll clean the upstairs bathroom three times a day instead of just two! I'll make dinner every night until I graduate from high school! Just please don't make me share a bathroom with him!"

"Calm down, Cindy," Dad said, patting her hand.

Mom went into the kitchen and came back out with one of those sponge things. She bent down to wipe up the soda Cynthia had spilled.

"I'll get that, Mom," Cynthia cried. She ran over, grabbed the sponge out of Mom's hand, and started rubbing the floor.

"What do you think, honey?" Dad asked Mom.

They looked at me as if I were a bug.

"I don't think it's quite fair, really—" Mom began.

Cynthia cut her off. "Fair! Fair? He won't clean up after himself! He won't put down the seat! That bathroom will be a gross mess in a day!"

37

A day? She wasn't giving me much credit. An hour was more like it.

"Still, sweetheart, I don't think it's fair to Joe. He'll just have to promise to try to be neater, that's all!" Mom insisted.

"It's okay, Mom," I announced, standing up. "If a clean bathroom is more important to Cynthia than our loving relationship, then I am prepared to sacrifice myself and be exiled to the basement bathroom!"

"Oh, for Pete's sake!" Cynthia exclaimed.

"No, no, don't feel sorry for me," I told them, holding my hands in the air. "I'll just go on down to the basement! Maybe I'll stay there. If I don't come back up, and ten years from now you go down there and see a dirty kid with ragged old clothes—that's me!"

"You're twelve," Mom said. "In ten years you'll be twenty-two."

"So?" I said. "What's your point?"

Mom threw her hands up in the air and said, "I give up!"

Cynthia said, "Mom, Dad, can I bring some of my Darling Debbie accessories into the bathroom? It's just a few things—just the towel rack and the cup and the toothbrush holder and makeup mirror..."

"Joe!" Mom called after me from the family room. I stopped in my tracks. Almost a clean getaway!

"Yeah?"

"You still have to keep it clean down there," she warned.

"Okay, Mom!" I called back. Then I raced down the basement stairs two at a time. I ran across the musty, cluttered basement, pulled open the door, and there it was.

My very own bathroom!

What more could a guy want?

Except his own house. His own car. A thorough pounding of Lumpy Leudke. Total world domination...the usual.

I was downstairs hanging up my Wolverine poster in the bathroom when Mom called down that it was time for bed.

It was a good thing we had two bathrooms. Wolverine vs. Darling Debbie—now there's a fight I'd like to see!

Before I left, I looked around the bathroom and thought about all the cool water fights and junk I was going to have down there with Roger. Then I turned out the lights and went upstairs.

Everybody was already in bed. I crept up the stairs to the second floor.

I was just starting down the hall toward my room when a weird sound started coming from the upstairs bathroom. It was like a giant toilet flushing.

I stopped.

A bright neon light was shining out from under the door—greenish yellow, almost. I tiptoed up to the door and was about to open it, when I heard my dad's voice saying, "I will get everything ready for transport."

Transport what? Who was he talking to?

Suddenly, the light disappeared. A second later, the door opened. My dad just stood there, a goofy, bland expression on his face. "What are you doing, Joey?"

Joey? He hadn't called me that in years. "Nothing, Dad. What was that bright light?" I asked. "And who were you talking to?"

"I wasn't talking to anyone, Joey," he told me.

"Oh. I thought you said something about transporting something. Were you singing?"

Dad rolled his eyes in this really strange way and nodded. "Yes, I was singing in the shower."

Funny. I hadn't heard the shower. "Are you sure?"

"Yes! Now go to bed, Joey!" he ordered.

"Dad, are you...all right?" I asked.

"I am one hundred percent intact."

Intact? What was that supposed to mean? Spending all that time in the sun doing yard work was warping my dad's brain!

I rolled over and looked at the clock. 1:24 A.M.

I couldn't sleep. I kept thinking about the light and sounds coming from the bathroom. And how my dad was saying things like "transport" and "intact."

Did it have something to do with the new toilet? Aunt Thelma had warned Dad not to buy it from that Gleepnorp guy. But everybody said she was wacko.

I had to check out the bathroom. I got out of bed really quietly and tiptoed down the hall. The bathroom door was shut. I turned the handle as softly as I could and crept inside. Then I closed the door and switched on the light.

"Aaahhh!" I screamed.

Darling Debbie—everywhere! Once I got over the shock, I walked over to the toilet. It was just sitting there, looking like...a toilet, basically.

What could a toilet do anyway?

I looked down into the bowl—just water.
Nothing special there. I reached out and put
my hand on the handle—and pushed it
down.

Nothing happened. No flush!

I pushed the handle down again and
again.

Dude! I'd only been in the stupid bathroom two seconds and I'd already broken the
stupid new toilet.

Suddenly the door swung open.

Dad!

"Listen, Dad, I'm sleepwalking!" I started
to explain. I didn't think he was going to buy
it, but I had to say something. "And you
know how dangerous it is to wake a sleep-
walker up, so I'll just head back to bed now.
Good night!"

"What are you doing in here, Joey?" he
asked in a cold voice.

That was it—I had to throw myself on the
mercy of the court!

"I am *so sorry*, Dad. I know I shouldn't be
in here! But I didn't break the new toilet—
I swear! I barely touched it!"

Dad smiled, but his eyes were kind of
empty-looking, as if they were made of glass.
I guess he was pretty tired.

"Break the new toilet? Of course you didn't, Joey. It is one hundred percent intact," he said.

"I don't know, but when I tried to flush it just now, it wouldn't flush," I explained.

Dad just kept on smiling at me. Then he said, "Of course it flushes—it's brand-new."

He walked past me to the toilet. He lifted the top, put his hand inside, and fiddled with something. Then he pushed down the handle. *Flush...gurgle...*

How come it hadn't worked for me?

"See that? The new toilet's just fine," he told me. "One hundred percent—"

Don't say it! I felt like screaming.

"Intact. And so are we all!"

I nodded. "Sure, Dad." He sounded like a greeting card or an after-school special.

Whatever! I went back to bed, but it was a long time before I could fall asleep. I tried telling myself a story.

Once upon a time there was this weird family—and then they started acting even weirder!

"Pass the Fruity-Os, Cynthia," I said the next morning.

Mom was rushing around like usual.

Cynthia was trying to wipe off the table with a dishrag and eat breakfast at the same time, so she wouldn't leave a mess. I glared at her and dribbled milk off my spoon onto the table. She stuck out her tongue.

"Hey, Mom, where's Dad?" I asked as Mom came racing back through the kitchen with a curling iron in her hand.

Dad always ate breakfast with us. Today was the first day that I could remember that he wasn't there.

"He's out in the garage. He said he had a project he wanted to work on," she told me.

"What's the new project?" I asked, munching a big bite of cereal.

"I don't know. He was kind of mysterious about it. He said I would find out soon enough," she told me, fixing her collar.

"Mom, do you think Dad is acting kind of weird?" I asked her.

"Takes one to know one," Cynthia said as she scrubbed her cereal bowl in the sink.

"You must know them all then," I said.

"C'mon, you guys, cut it out," Mom said. She thought for a moment, then added, "He did seem real excited about this new thing he's doing in the garage—whatever it is. But you know how much your dad likes to work.

Between you and me, I think this vacation is driving him a little nutty."

A little nutty? I'll say!

Mom looked at her watch. "Oh, I really have to get going!"

She came over and kissed us both on the cheek.

Then we heard a long roll of thunder.

Mom went to the window. "It's pouring!" she cried. "That's odd. It was sunny when I got up."

"It's called a weather front," I said.

My mom didn't even hear me. She was muttering something about where she'd left our umbrellas. Then she snapped her fingers. "The basement!" She walked over to the basement stairs and disappeared.

I poured myself another bowl of cereal. It was still only seven-thirty. I didn't have to be out for the bus until a quarter past eight.

All of a sudden...

"Eeeeeeek!"

A scream—from the basement!

CHAPTER
6

"Mom!" I cried, rushing down the stairs.

"Mother!" Cynthia yelled, following me.

I stopped and gave Cynthia a look. "You've never called her 'Mother' before."

"*Hello?* When people are in trouble, you have to show them a little more respect!"

We practically trampled each other getting to the bottom of the stairs.

"What is it, Mother? What's wrong!" Cynthia cried.

"Is it another possum?" I asked.

One time, Mom saw this huge possum in the basement. She thought it was a giant rat!

She turned around and glared at me. "How in the world could you have made a mess like this in just one night?" she demanded, jabbing her finger at my stomach.

I smiled. "Well, it wasn't easy."

She threw her hands in the air. "You're impossible, Joe! If you think I'm cleaning up that mess, you're dead wrong, mister! Now you get that bathroom cleaned up!"

"Okay with me, Mom. I don't mind if I miss the school bus. As a matter of fact, why don't I drop out of school altogether. I have a lot of TV watching to catch up on."

Mom walked over to me, swinging her arms back and forth to look tough. "You will go to school, young man. And then you will come home and you will clean up this bathroom. Do you understand me?"

"Sure, Mom—no problem!" I assured her.

She wagged her finger at me. "I mean it, Joe. You'll be in big trouble if you don't!"

Cynthia crept over and peeked into the bathroom. "Totally gross!" she shrieked. She ran past Mom and me and up the stairs.

Even if Mom was mad, seeing Cynthia freak was worth it!

Everybody knew I was supposed to fight Lumpy after school on Monday. And everybody was waiting behind the backstop when Roger and I showed up.

Lumpy was actually late. I was starting to

think that he wasn't going to show.

I wished he would. I was really in the mood for a fight. I'd just gotten out of English class.

I hate English. My teacher is Mr. Hunt. He's this big guy with the bushiest eyebrows in the world. He has this nasty habit of sneaking up behind you if you're fooling around and not working. Then he whacks you in the back of the head with his thumb—and it's the biggest thumb in the world, I swear. I've checked out a lot of them.

And since I mess around a lot in class, I get whacked by the Thumb—that's what we call Mr. Hunt—a lot.

"Hey, there's Lumpy," Roger whispered to me.

Lumpy walked onto the playground. He didn't look too good.

Excellent, I thought. There's nothing better than winning without even trying. That's what all the great coaches say.

"He looks sick," said Roger.

"So would you, if you were fighting me," I told him. I hate to brag, but—

No, I don't. What am I thinking? I love to brag. It's my life!

A bunch of guys were slapping Lumpy on

the back. But he was just holding his stomach and shaking his head. His face looked kind of green, almost as bad a shade as Aunt Thelma's pantsuit from the other day at the toilet store.

"I think he's probably faking because he's scared of me," I said. "Maybe we should call the fight off."

Roger gave me a look of total disgust. "Bawk, bawk."

"I'm not chicken!" I protested.

"You are so!" he insisted.

"I am not!" That did it. Nobody calls me a chicken and gets away with it, not even my best friend. I was really going to have to beat Lumpy up now—in a big way!

I marched across the grass to where Lumpy was standing, rubbing his stomach and moaning.

"So, Lumpmeister, are you ready to go for it?" I challenged.

Lumpy just groaned.

Donald Blauvelt stepped out from behind Lumpy. Donald is Lumpy's sidekick. He's a skinny little kid, but he's really mean.

"He's sick," Donald told me. "Can't fight."

"Oh, little Lumpy-Wumpy's all sickywicky," I sneered.

"He was in the nurse's office all afternoon," Donald told me.

"Yeah, I'll bet. What did he have, a nervous breakdown? Joe Kohler's going to get me! Help me, Nurse. Help me!" I taunted.

Lumpy lifted his head and looked at me. He really did look sort of sick. I'd heard about people turning green, but I'd never really seen it before. Lumpy's a big guy—bigger than me—with a big round face and really short red hair. He stared at me for a minute and then he kind of burped out, "That's it, Joe-Joe!"

Joe-Joe! Remember what I said about that name? That's why we were fighting in the first place! Nobody gets to call me Joe-Joe—except Aunt Thelma!

I put my fists up. "All right, man—you're on!"

Lumpy put his fists up and glared at me. He looked really tired, though, like he was having trouble holding his fists in the air.

We circled around each other. Everybody was yelling junk like "Kick his butt, Lumpy!" or "Pound him, Joe!"

Lumpy threw a punch at me, but it seemed as if it was in slow motion. Then his face got even greener. And he fell forward—right into my arms! He started groaning really loudly.

I looked down at his face.

It couldn't be. He wasn't going to. He wouldn't.

He did!

Lumpy collapsed. His last words after he puked were, "Do you give?"

Then he passed out.

Lumpy's friends picked him up and started running for the nurse's office. I looked down at my shirt.

Spew—all over me! Fight *over*, dude! Disgusting!

There was only one thing to do.

I ran as fast as I could all the way home.

I heard Roger yelling for me to wait up, but I couldn't. I had to get home and wash off. Immediately! Like yesterday!

I got home, ran down to the basement, and got in the shower. I felt as if I needed to go through the car wash, or the *monster truck* wash.

Dude, I have been in some *bad* fights in my life, but...barf fighting? Totally unfair! His nickname ought to be Chunky instead of Lumpy if he was going to fight like that.

When I was totally clean, I went upstairs and lay down on my bed. Sorry, Mom, but cleaning up the basement bathroom was going to have to wait.

I was staring up at the ceiling when I started to feel sort of sick. All of a sudden my stomach started twisting up and jumping around. And then I felt it...

The Big Spew!

I must've caught the same disease Lumpy had. Germ warfare! Man, Lumpy played rough.

I tried to talk my stomach out of it. "Now then, Mr. Stomach, let's be reasonable. We both have our jobs to do. My job is to feed you, which I think I do pretty well. And your job is to keep whatever I give you down there."

I promised it all sorts of goodies if it would just keep cool during this crisis time. Twinkies, Ho-Hos, Peanut-Butter-and Gummi-Worm ice cream...

It was working. My stomach settled down for a minute. But it was a trick. I was definitely going to spew!

I jumped out of bed.

There was no time to lose—no way I could make it to the basement.

I had no choice. I had to use the forbidden bathroom!

I ran out of my room and down the hall. I flung the bathroom door open. I could almost hear Darling Debbie laughing at me as I bent over the toilet bowl to get sick.

Whatever it was that Lumpy had, now it was mine!

I must have knelt there talking on the porcelain telephone for fifteen minutes before I could even raise my head. And then, finally, I reached up to flush.

I kept my head down, fingering my way up the cold toilet tank until I felt the smooth, metal handle under my fingers.

And then I pulled.

Ka-chunk!

"Owwwwww!"

The toilet seat had slammed down—pinning me to the toilet!

It was trying to cut my head off!

Then, suddenly, the bathroom started getting really cold. It wasn't like a wind or anything. The temperature just dropped to an arctic level!

"What's the deal, man?" I cried, but my voice disappeared into the swirling water.

Then a bright light started coming out of

the bowl—and the water started rising with it! It was getting higher and higher, and the greenish neon light glowed brighter and brighter.

Just like I'd seen last night, when my dad was in here!

I struggled to get away from the toilet, but the seat held me too tight! The water kept rising. I was going to drown!

What was with this dumb new toilet?!

I used all my strength to get away from it, pulling and pushing against the seat, which was jamming my head against the bowl. The light got so bright, I wanted to shield my eyes. But my face was trapped under the toilet seat, so I couldn't reach them!

Then I saw it—a face staring at me out of the toilet. It had a tiny mouth and these little beady red eyes! But who was it? It looked like Darling Debbie!

The face got closer and closer. It was screaming at me!

I put all my strength into one final shove—and finally pushed the toilet seat back long enough to get my head out.

I leaned back against the wall, panting and staring at the evil toilet. Some sanitary unit!

"What's going on in our bathroom?" I moaned.

"That's what I'd like to know," a voice replied on the other side of the door.

CHAPTER

7

Mom walked into the bathroom, and her eyes went wide. "Sweetheart, what's the matter? Were you having a light show in here? Oh, my gosh, you look terrible!"

I held myself up by grasping the door. "Is my face hurting you?" I asked.

Mom took me by the arm and led me to my room. "Of course your face isn't hurting me, honey."

"Well, it's killing me," I croaked, rubbing my cheek. I could feel a bruise already forming where the seat had slammed me.

My mom helped me into bed. She gazed down at me with a concerned look. "What happened?"

I was about to tell her when Roger came running into my room. "Lumpy Leudke totally spewed all over him, Mrs. Kohler!"

"Thank you, Roger," said Mom. "That was nice and graphic. I appreciate it." Then she turned to me. "Is this true, Joe?"

I nodded. That much was true—but the behavior of our weird new toilet was worrying me a lot more than Lumpy!

"Well, I know there's a bad twenty-four hour stomach virus going around. At least it's not serious. Do you want some 7-Up? It'll settle your stomach." She felt my forehead. "My goodness, I think you have a little fever."

"Could I have some ice cream, too?" I asked

Mom frowned. "No. How about some saltines?"

I could be dying, and my mother wouldn't give me anything good to eat. "Okay."

"I'll be right back," she said, heading downstairs.

As soon as she was gone, I turned to Roger. "Rog, listen. Something really weird happened—"

"I know, man! Lumpy was totally sick."

"Not that, dude. Something happened in the bathroom," I began.

"Yeah. You puked!" Roger interrupted.

"No!" I yelled. "I'm talking about that new toilet! It tried to kill me!"

Roger looked at me for a minute. Then he said, "You really *are* sick."

"Roger, I'm telling the truth—that is not a normal toilet. My dad was in there last night, and he's been acting weird ever since! He calls me Joey and he didn't even eat breakfast with us, which he always does!"

"Man, that *is* weird!" Roger agreed. "Your dad eats breakfast with you? My dad says he can't stand to see me before lunchtime!"

"Forget about that, dude!" I shouted at him in total frustration. "I'm telling you, there's definitely something sinister about that toilet!"

Just then, my mom walked in with the soda and crackers.

"What about the toilet?" she asked

"Mom, I don't know what happened exactly, but I think the new toilet tried to murder me," I told her.

She frowned and felt my head. "You don't feel that warm, honey."

I sat up and looked her right in the face. "I mean it, Mom! The toilet tried to cut my head off with the seat. And the water was swirling up, trying to suck me in and drown me! And then—I know you're going to think this is crazy—but I saw this ugly, horrible face in the toilet. It wasn't even human!"

Mom shook her head. "I believe you think you saw something in the bathroom. You could have imagined something not-human, like you say—"

"But, Mom—!"

"Or it could've been your own reflection," she said.

"Same thing," Roger joked.

I glared at him. "But, Mom, it was so real!" I insisted. "And Dad is acting weird—he keeps calling me Joey!"

"He's not acting weird, Joe. He's just excited. I talked to him a few minutes ago."

"Did he say anything about being one hundred percent intact?" I demanded.

She shook her head. "No. As a matter of fact, I didn't see him. He talked to me through the garage door," she said.

"There, you see?" I cried. "He won't even come out!"

"What's the matter with you, Joe? I saw your father last night and he was fine. He said he didn't want to open the garage door because he's planning a surprise for all of us and we have to wait until he's finished to see it. Now, just to prove to you that there's nothing wrong with the new toilet, I'm going in there to get cleaned up!" Mom announced.

She stood up and smoothed her skirt. "That is, of course, unless you need anything else?" she asked. "More saltines, maybe?"

"No, Mom." I was still trying to swallow the last one she'd fed me. "I'm fine."

"All right then, I'll see you in a little bit," she said. Then she left my room.

We were silent as she went into the bathroom and we heard the door close. I didn't think she should go in there, but I was too sick and weak to stop her.

Anyway, if she didn't want to believe me, maybe now she'd get her proof. We needed to return that toilet to Floville—immediately! I had enough problems without getting killed by a toilet seat.

"You believe me, don't you, Rog?" I asked.

"I think you're acting like a nut!" he said.

"Well, you know what I think? You are the geek of all time!" I shot back at him.

"Oh, yeah—" he began. "Hey, what's that?" Roger asked.

"That's the flush of the killer toilet!" I cried.

I jumped out of bed and ran down the hall. Roger was right behind me. I got to the door and started pounding as hard as I could.

"Mom!" I cried. "Are you all right? Please, Mom, answer me! Say something!"

Finally, the door swung open. Mom stood there wearing her bathrobe, with her hair wrapped up in a towel. She glared down at me. Giant clouds of steam rolled out the bathroom door.

"Are you okay, Mom?" I asked.

She had a funny expression on her face.

"Joey! What's the matter, Joey? Roger! How nice to see you, Roger!" she said.

She was calling me Joey—just like Dad!

"Are you okay, Mom?" I asked again.

"Of course I'm okay, Joey. Are you still worried about the new toilet? Now, you listen to me—there's nothing wrong with that toilet!"

"Sure, Mom," I said. "Whatever you say."

She patted me on the head and smiled. "Good, I'm glad that's settled. Now, you boys sure look hungry. How would you guys like some delicious homemade chocolate chip cookies?" she asked. "On top of some fudge ripple ice cream? A little hot fudge, some delicious non-dairy whipped topping, too?"

"Yeah!" Roger and I cried.

Then it hit me. She didn't sound like the Mom I knew at all.

"Wait a second," I said. "You just said I shouldn't have ice cream. I'm sick, remember?"

"Sick?" Mom looked perplexed. "You look fine to me."

"But, I just threw up!" I said. I wished I could forget as quickly as she had.

"Oh, that was hours ago. I'm sure you're peachy now. I'll get dressed and start baking!"

Mom used to make homemade cookies, but ever since she started going back to school, she hasn't really had time. "But, Mom, don't you have to study tonight?"

She bent down and smiled in my face. "Law school's not that important!" she said. Then she walked past us, down the hall, to her bedroom.

"Come on, Rog," I said, grabbing Roger's arm. "There's something not normal about all of this. We have to check it out. I think that toilet stole my mother!" I pushed the bathroom door open and snapped on the light.

"It's horrible—Darling Debbie every-where!" Roger cried.

"Oh, yeah. I forgot to warn you," I said.

We stood there silently for a minute and looked around.

"It just looks like a normal bathroom to me," Roger said, shrugging.

I had to admit that he was right. Except for the Darling Debbie stuff, it *did* look pretty normal.

But I knew something was wrong. There was something sinister going on in this bath-room, and my family was in danger.

"Shouldn't we get out of here? Your folks don't want you in here, right?" Roger said, glancing out into the hallway.

I turned to him. "That's right, they don't want me in here. And that's exactly why I have to be in here! Now guard the door," I ordered him. I walked over to the toilet and stared at it.

Nothing happened.

Then I remembered what Dad had done the other night. I felt around behind the toi-let tank, but it was smooth and cold—just like normal. I reached further down. I don't know what I was looking for, but there had to be *something* weird. I ran my hand all over the porcelain, and...there it was!

A tiny seam or crack. I ran my finger along it. It was a miniature trapdoor!

"Hey, Roger, c'mere," I whispered.

Roger checked the hall again to make sure no one was coming, and then he joined me by the toilet.

"I don't like this, Joe," he said. "We could get in big trouble being in here!"

"I'm sick, remember? We'll just say I started throwing up again." I found the little door again and put his hand on the seam. "Feel that? What do you think it is?"

"I don't know—what is it?" he asked.

"I saw my dad fooling with something back here last night. Probably whatever it was is behind this panel," I told him.

"Well...maybe there's a secret button around here somewhere," Roger said.

"Yeah, just like in Armies of Evil!" I exclaimed.

Then I remembered the other part of the secret interactive option in Armies of Evil. Sometimes the secret buttons were booby-trapped. If you hit the wrong one—*KA-BOOM!*

Roger was twisting bolts and things, trying to remove the back panel from the toilet.

"Be careful," I warned him. "Remember that time we were fighting in the Omega system, and I had your second squadron surrounded, and you pushed that secret option?" I asked, hoping I wouldn't have to jump on his head to jog his memory.

Roger was taking forever. I got totally impatient and pushed him out of the way. Then I ran my hand over the back of the toilet again. Maybe I had missed something. I was about to give up when I felt a little switch. I pushed it. There was a whirring sound—and then the panel opened.

"I got it!" I announced. "Look!"

We peered into the space between the toilet tank and the wall. We saw a blinking light, and there was a bunch of buttons and switches.

Roger looked up at me with a panicked expression. "Dude, this is not a normal toilet!"

Just then, the bathroom door was yanked open from the outside!

CHAPTER
8

"Cynthia!" Roger gasped.

"Yeah—so? What are you two doing in here?" She stood there in her cheerleading uniform. Her hair was in two tightly tied ponytails. Maybe that was her problem—they were probably *too* tight and squeezing her brain.

"We're not doing anything," I said.

Cynthia turned from me to Roger and back to me. Then she shook her head. "So what are you waiting for? An invitation? Get out! You're not supposed to be in here."

She reached under the sink and brought out a can of Darling Debbie Disinfectant Spray. She held the can up and started spraying the bathroom.

"What are you doing?" I asked her.

"I'm killing germs on contact," she

explained. "I don't know what you dweebs have been doing in here, but I'm sure you didn't check your microbes at the door. Now get out of here before you contaminate everything again!"

Should I tell her or keep the parental problem under raps? I didn't even know what was going on. What could I tell her anyway?

"Let's go, Rog," I said.

Cynthia was tapping her foot and glaring at us. Roger looked at me and then back at Cynthia.

"But Joe..." he said.

"What? What can we do? She'd never believe us anyway!" I told him, shaking my head. What a dorkus!

"But we have to tell her, Joe!" Roger cried.

I knew he sort of had a crush on her. But man! Did he want to warn her or something? I kind of *liked* the idea of the killer toilet hitting Cynthia on the head.

"Tell me what?" she demanded. "Are you two dweebs hiding something?"

I stepped up to her. "First of all, we are *not* dweebs. Second of all, we're *not* hiding anything. It's that thing!" I said, pointing at the toilet.

"The new sanitary unit is hiding things?"

"Yes," I said. "I mean no. It's not hiding things. It's...it's...alive!"

"Well, *that's* nice." She shook her head. "What in the world is going on in your head?"

"It's a killer toilet! Haven't you noticed how strange Dad is acting? He hasn't come out of the garage for days! And do you know what Mom's going to do this afternoon?"

Cynthia shrugged. "No, what?"

"She's going to make cookies!" I burst out.

Cynthia's mouth fell open. "But...that's impossible! That can't be!" she gasped, steadying herself against the medicine cabinet. "Mom doesn't have time to bake! She has to study! And work! If she doesn't make it through law school...I don't know what'll happen to us! She hasn't baked cookies in...three years!"

"Now all of a sudden she says she has all the time in the world!" I told her.

"And you think that Mom and Dad acting bizarre has something to do with that...that thing?" she asked.

Roger went over to the toilet and felt around behind it. "There is definitely something weird here, Cynthia. I didn't believe it either, but then we found—" He moved his hand around a little faster and began to look worried. "We found these buttons and things and switches and junk and—" His hand groped even more frantically, and then he looked at me. "They're gone!" he announced.

"What?" I ran over and shoved Roger out of the way. He was right—there was no trace of the buttons and switches. I couldn't even feel the seam anymore.

Cynthia was going to think I was totally nuts. *I* was starting to think I was.

"You found what?" Cynthia demanded, peering back behind the tank.

"Uh...never mind. Nothing. Just a little joke to brighten your day, Cynthia—ha, ha!"

"But, Joe, it was there—I saw it!" Roger insisted.

"What is he talking about, Joe?" Cynthia asked.

"Oh, you know Roger—who knows what he's talking about? Right? What are you talking about, Roger?"

He looked puzzled for a minute. Then he started playing along. "Me? Uh, nothing—nothing at all!" We both laughed really loudly and smiled.

"You guys are so strange," Cynthia said as we backed out the door.

"Good-bye, Cynthia—bye-bye!" I told her. She slammed the door in our faces, and Roger and I ran back to my room.

I turned on my stereo and Roger and I just looked at each other. After a while I started feeling pretty sick again. My stomach felt as if somebody was squeezing and unsqueezing it like an accordion. I lay down, and Roger said he had to leave.

"Okay, dude, see you tomorrow in school," I told him.

"Okay," he replied. "See ya!" I heard the front door close a minute later.

I was just starting to relax when my mom came into my room, carrying a tray.

"Mom? Are you all right? I mean, you feel okay, don't you?"

She smiled and brushed her brown hair out of her eyes. "Sure I'm okay, Joey. Don't I seem okay?" she asked.

"No, you don't!" I told her. "All of a sudden you're making cookies and calling me Joey like you used to when I was a kid!"

"Don't you want me to make cookies for you?" she asked me.

"Sure I do. But you always say you don't

have time to do stuff like that anymore. And now all of a sudden you do."

"You're worth it, Joey! Now, would you like me to read you a bedtime story?" she asked.

I shook my head. "Mom, I'm *twelve*. Nobody reads stories to me anymore."

"Oh." She looked disappointed. "Well then, how about if I bring the TV in so you can watch *Sesame Street*?"

My mother's brain was stuck in some kind of time warp. Maybe she'd been working too many hours or something, I tried to tell myself. "No, thanks, Mom." I said. "I think I'll just sleep."

"Nighty-night, Joey!" she whispered.

My mom was losing her mind!

I woke up abruptly in the middle of the night.

Someone was knocking at my door!

It was really dark in my room. My digital clock said it was three-thirty in the morning.

Who would be knocking at my bedroom door at three-thirty in the morning?

"Who is it?" I asked.

I jumped out of bed and ran over to the door. I pulled it open. Nobody was there.

What was going on? "Maybe I dreamed the whole thing," I muttered out loud, rubbing my eyes.

Then I heard it. A gurgle.

There came the sound of wrenching metal and rushing water. No! Not the toilet! Had it gotten Cynthia now, too?

There was a kind of thumping sound, like somebody walking toward me with really heavy feet.

"Cynthia?" I whispered.

But it wasn't Cynthia.

It was the new toilet—coming out of the bathroom and heading straight toward me, lighting up the hallway with its neon glow!

I backed into my room and slammed my bedroom door shut. I stood near my bed, my legs shaking with fear. The toilet crashed through my door and kept right on coming!

Why did I have to be born into a family of heavy sleepers? Nobody was going to come save me!

The toilet backed me up against the wall. Then it opened its lid. Water and light were churning around inside—and it started sucking things into it!

All my books went flying off my shelf and into the toilet. Then all my—

Not my comics! Not Wolverine!

I grabbed my stack of comics and tried to dodge around the toilet.

It was trying to suck me in, too! The vacuum got stronger and stronger. Slowly it began to pull me into its horrible depths. I got closer and closer—

Then I saw the face—the same one I had seen before! It was just as ugly, and it was laughing at me!

"Nice to see you again, Joe!" it gurgled.

"You'll never get me!" I cried. I leaped over the toilet, ran out of my room, and dashed downstairs to the basement. I hurried into the bathroom down there and locked the door, looking up at Wolverine for good luck.

I'd like to see that toilet get down the stairs without falling and breaking into a hundred pieces.

I leaned against Wolverine, panting and heaving. I'm not in very good shape, I guess.

Then again, I don't exactly practice escaping killer toilets in gym class. I let out a deep sigh and sat down on the bathtub.

That's when I realized I was sitting in the same room with another toilet!

But this one wasn't a killer. I glanced at it nervously. Or was it?

CHAPTER
9

I woke up on the bathroom floor, my face pressed into the terry bath mat. I pulled a cotton ball off my lip.

Then I remembered why I was sleeping in the basement! I jumped up and cautiously opened the door. No killer toilet.

I had to go upstairs and get ready for school. I took the steps two at a time. When I passed the upstairs bathroom, the door was closed. There was no evidence that the toilet had been out in the hall, running after me. No pieces of broken porcelain. No shards of wood. No water-soaked carpet.

But the door was closed. That meant somebody was in there with...It!

I ran to my room and closed the door. I changed clothes as quickly as I could. For once I couldn't wait to get to school!

I was almost ready when there was a knock at the door. "You can't come in!" I yelled.

"I don't want to!" Cynthia replied.

"Cynthia? Is that really you?" I asked suspiciously. If a toilet could walk, it could probably imitate voices, too.

"Who do you think it is, ding-dong?" Cynthia shouted through the door. "Mom told me to tell you you're going to be late!"

Phew! It wasn't the sinister toilet! It was just a dorky sister!

"Okay, Miss Neat Freak," I said.

Things were getting really weird. I was actually glad to talk to Cynthia. "Hey, how's Mister Clean and all your little scrubbing bubbles?" I asked, opening the door.

Cynthia was about to start down the stairs!

"Cynthia!" I cried, horrified.

She turned around. "What?" she demanded, her hands on her hips.

I almost fell over from shock.

Her outfit. And her hair! She looked the way she used to when she was a tomboy and spent her whole day climbing trees. Back when she was *cool*.

"Come here a second," I said.

Cynthia sighed loudly and then walked toward me. I looked her up and down. She was wearing cut-off jeans shorts that had stuff written on them. Her T-shirt was wrinkled, as if she'd picked it up off the floor.

I started shaking all over. Her T-shirt wasn't even tucked in!

And her hair! It was as if she'd slicked it down with cooking oil.

"You look pale," I said. "Are you feeling all right?"

"I'm feeling better than you look," Cynthia retorted.

"Don't bet on it," I said. Then I realized... she wasn't wearing any makeup! She didn't have the familiar aroma of Darling Debbie Devastating Eau de Cologne. She didn't even have her Darling Debbie Dee-lightful Deodorant on. (I could tell because it always stinks up the whole house.)

"What are you looking at?" she asked.

"I was just wondering...you used the bathroom last night, didn't you? I mean, you took a shower and you were in there for a while...right?"

"Yes, Joe," she said, rolling her eyes.

"Listen," I pleaded. "This is serious, Cynthia. Did you notice anything strange about the toilet last night?"

"What is your problem? You have sanitary units on the brain or something," she said. "No, there was nothing funny about it—now get dressed or you're going to miss breakfast!" She turned and headed for the stairs.

First that toilet had gotten my dad. Then my mom. Now my sister, too!

Good thing I was able to resist it. Hey, why change? I'm perfect the way I am.

Still, I wasn't sure how I would live with a bunch of wackos. I'd think of something.

I hummed the theme from Armies of Evil as I finished getting ready for school, hoping it would inspire me. I tied my sneakers and grabbed my backpack. I still had twenty minutes until the bus came.

I went downstairs and walked into the kitchen.

"Dad!" I cried. "No! Don't do it!"

Dad was sitting at the table, polishing off the last slice of French toast.

My mom looked at him. Then she and Dad both looked at Cynthia. Cynthia nodded. Then Dad turned to me and smiled. "Good morning, Joey!" he boomed.

Major family conspiracy!

First, my dad was still calling me Joey.

Second, my mom hasn't made French toast, much less cinnamon raisin French toast with powdered sugar on top, since I was five. And third—oh, no! Cynthia was dribbling sticky maple syrup all over the tablecloth! And then she put her elbows in—the biggest mess she'd made in years!

"Dad, please don't call me Joey," I said. "Mom, Fruity-Os are just fine."

She smiled brightly. "How about banana walnut pancakes and a cheese soufflé?" She opened the refrigerator, which was suddenly packed with groceries, and started pulling out ingredients.

"Cynthia," I said, "watch your elbows!"

She looked at me as if I were crazy. Me, crazy! I was the only sane one!

I sat down at my place at the table, looking carefully at my dad. "What happened to your head?" I asked. He had a bandage on his forehead.

"Oh, it's nothing. I bumped it last night— no big deal," he told me.

"Does it hurt?" I asked.

"Not at all!" he told me, grinning. "My brain is one hundred percent intact."

His smile was weirding me out. Something was definitely wrong here. "Hey,

Dad. I was wondering if I could check out what you're doing in the garage," I asked him, trying to sound casual.

Dad stopped smiling and looked at Cynthia. Why did he keep looking at her? They hadn't been pals since she was eight.

"No, Joey, you can't!" he snapped. "That is...er...not yet. I want it to be a surprise!" He started smiling again.

"Well, when's it going to be done?" I asked.

"Soon enough, Joey...soon enough," he said in a low, mysterious voice that didn't sound like my dad's at all.

"Okay, Dad," I said.

Just then, Mom came over, carrying a plate with eight perfect, round pancakes on it. "Uh...I have to catch the bus in a few minutes anyway," I said. "I think I'll just get going."

"All right, sweetheart," she said. She wasn't even mad that I didn't want the food she made! That kind of stuff usually kills her.

I pushed back my chair. I couldn't get out of there fast enough!

"Sorry about breakfast, but look—I made you a nice lunch to bring with you to school!" Mom announced. She handed me a giant brown paper bag. It weighed about ten pounds!

I ran all the way to the bus stop. When I got there, I tossed my lunch into the trash. I was afraid of what she'd packed!

It's hard to concentrate in school when your family is possessed.

"I have to go back to that Gleepnorp's Sanitary Unit store and check it out," I whispered to Roger in English class.

The Thumb was across the room.

"It's really far away, man," Roger said.

"It's not that far," I told him.

"It would take us all day to get there on our bikes! It might even be dark before we got back," he argued.

I looked at him for a long time. Then I opened my eyes really wide and stared at him.

"What are you looking at?" he said.

"What did you do with my buddy Roger?" I asked. "One minute he was sitting here, and now there's a big, ugly chicken!"

"Shut up, geekbrain!" Roger begged. "The Thumb is going to hear you!"

"I don't care who hears me! You listen to me, you big chicken—"

Thump!

I turned around. The Thumb was smiling down at me. He held his thumb cocked and ready for another assault. It really is the biggest thumb in the history of the world.

I bet Mr. Hunt used to be in the circus or something. The Incredible, Amazing Thumb.

"What was that you were saying, Mr. Kohler?" he asked me.

"Nothing, Mr. Hunt," I said, trying to look innocent. "Roger and I were just—"

Thump!

"Ow! What was that for?" I asked, rubbing the back of my head.

"Well, Mr. Kohler, if you were saying nothing, then I guess that was for nothing," Mr. Hunt announced. Then he leaned down close and whispered in my ear. "Just wait and see what happens if I catch you saying something."

He's really funny, that Mr. Hunt.

About as funny as my report card.

"Then it's agreed." I said. "Next Saturday, you and I are going to ride our bikes back to that sanitary unit store and check it out."

Roger nodded. It was after school, and we were both staring at the upstairs bathroom door, which now had a large padlock on it.

"This toilet problem is totally cutting into our Armies of Evil playing time," Roger complained.

"Tell me about it," I agreed.

I reached out and pulled on the padlock. Whatever was going on in that bathroom was now officially off-limits to me.

"It wasn't locked this morning," I said.

"Well, it's locked now!" Cynthia said, suddenly coming out of her bedroom.

Roger jumped. He was shocked—who wouldn't be?

Cynthia looked so...different!

Her hair was all messed up, and she wasn't wearing any Darling Debbie Young 'n' Fresh Makeup.

"What's the matter with you?" I asked her as she came down the hall toward us.

"What do you mean, what's the matter with me?" she asked. She stopped and looked down at herself.

"Your hair—it's all tangled," I said.

She pushed her hair back behind her ears and smiled. "Oh, well. So, how do you like the 'No-Fault Dorky Little Brother Protection Device' I installed?" she asked, tapping the lock.

"Mom and Dad let you put a lock on the bathroom door?" I asked her.

She grinned. "Yeah!" she said happily.

Then I remembered something that had been drilled into me for the last two years.

No not putting down the seat.

"Hey, aren't you supposed to be at cheerleader practice?" I asked her.

"Cheerleading?" Cynthia scoffed. "Right, as if!" She looked confused for a minute, then she frowned at me. "Am I?" she asked.

"Yeah—every day at five-thirty," I told her.

She looked at us suspiciously for a minute. Then she laughed. "Of course I am, dorkus. I was just testing you!"

"Oh," I replied.

"Well, I'll see you two geeks later—I have to get ready for practice!" she announced, as if it was really big news.

"Yeah...you do that!" I called after her as she disappeared down the hall.

When she was safely back in her room, I studied the lock again. Then I looked at Roger.

"C'mon dude—I'm going to find out what's going on!" I said.

Roger followed me downstairs and out

the sliding glass door.

"I thought we were going to play Armies of Evil," he whined.

"Don't worry. I have a feeling we're going to be living it," I told him as I led him around to the backyard.

I walked up to the side window of the garage and tried to look inside. I couldn't see anything. The window was covered with dark paper. So we walked around to the other window in the back.

"What's that noise?" Roger asked as we tramped through the grass.

There was a continuous hum coming from the garage. It sounded like a giant window fan blowing. I could hear voices, too. It sounded as if Dad was talking to somebody!

Who could he be talking to? I walked up to the window and tried to look inside again. This window was blacked out, too, but there was a little crack of light along the lower edge of the glass. I bent over and peered inside.

"What do you see, dude?" Roger asked.

I couldn't see much. I saw my dad's legs for a minute. There was something in there—something big but I couldn't tell what it was. I leaned a little closer.

All of a sudden, something was looking right back at me!

"*Aaaaahhhhhhhhhh!*" I cried, falling backward onto the grass. "There was an eye!" I screamed to Roger. "It looked at me—in the window! It was horrible!"

"Joey—Roger! What are you two boys doing?" a voice demanded.

A monster in a space suit and helmet was coming out of the garage—straight toward us!

CHAPTER
10

Roger and I both screamed at the top of our lungs.

Then the monster took off its helmet. It was my mom!

"Mom, what are you doing home?" I asked. "You're supposed to be at work!"

Mom just glared at us. "A better question, young man, is what are you doing out here snooping around?"

"I'm not snooping," I insisted. "Why are you wearing that *space* suit?"

"It's not a space suit, Joe. It s a welding suit! I'm helping your father!" she told me.

"Helping him with what, Mom?" I cried. "Why is the bathroom door locked? What's going on?"

Suddenly my mom smiled. "How would

you like some delicious cookies, Joey?"

Huh?

"My name's not Joey, and I don't want any cookies!" I insisted. "I want to know what's going on!"

"You'll know soon enough. Everyone will know soon enough," she said mysteriously, glancing up at the sky.

Then she looked at us again. "Now run along!"

"Okay, Mom!" I said. I grabbed Roger and we backed away.

"Gee, I've never heard your mom sound so tough before," Roger said. "She's kind of scary."

"And she hasn't stopped making cookies and pies ever since we got that new killer toilet!" I said. "Something's very, very wrong!"

That night, I tried to call Aunt Thelma. I thought if anybody would know what was going on, she would. But she was never home. I left about a hundred messages for her, but she never called back.

Was she dead or what?

Or maybe she *had* moved to that trash can after all.

I had to get to Floville and find out!

* * *

"They're gone!" I cried, looking in the window of what had been Gleepnorp's Sanitary Units and Appliances.

Roger and I had ridden all day to get to Floville—and the store was deserted! Shut down. There was no sign—nothing—no evidence that there had ever been a Gleepnorp store at all!

I tried the door. It was locked tight. I decided to walk around to the back to see if there was a back entrance.

When I turned the corner, I stopped dead in my tracks.

Roger, who was walking right behind me, ran into me, and we knocked heads.

"What are you doing, pinhead?" I asked him.

"Why'd you stop so fast, mushbrain?" he shot back at me.

"*I'm* not the mushbrain!" I retorted.

"Great comeback, dorkus!" he said.

I was about to burn him good by talking about his nose. He broke it two years ago when he tried to fly off his roof, using a beach umbrella as a parachute.

But I didn't say anything. Because, just then I saw the last thing in the world that I wanted to see...

Aunt Thelma's bike!

"That's my aunt's bike!" I told Roger, pointing.

Then I realized something else—the old burned-out white car thing that looked like a broken-down spaceship was gone! There were just some marks on the pavement, like tire tracks when someone screeches to a stop and burns rubber.

Suddenly two pictures formed in my mind. I saw the car-thing, and I heard Aunt Thelma telling me to get away from it.

Then I saw our new toilet—and I realized why I thought I had seen the car-thing before! It looked like a toilet! It was round up front—and square in the back. It didn't look exactly like a toilet, but it was close enough.

And where did that weird Gleepnorp say he was from again?

"Polaris!" I cried. Suddenly it all became clear.

Aunt Thelma had disappeared, along with the toilet-shaped spaceship...my family's brains had turned to mush...my family had probably gone into space *with* Aunt Thelma, while I was hanging around Floville, doing nothing!

I ran back to my bike. "Come on, man!" I called over my shoulder.

Roger ran up beside me and we both got on our bikes and started pedaling.

"Where're you going so fast?" he asked.

"Rog, we have to get back right now," I told him. "My family's been kidnapped by aliens!"

An hour later, I dropped my bike on the lawn and raced into the house. Roger was right behind me.

"Mom! Dad! Cynthia! Where are you?" I cried, panting. The ride usually took us three hours. We'd practically flown home.

The television was on in the living room, but nobody was watching it. Bad sign. The family room was empty and eerie. It didn't even seem like my house anymore. It was full of some weird unearthly presence.

"Do you really think your whole family was kidnapped by aliens in the toilet?" Roger asked. "Maybe you've been playing too much Armies of Evil."

"Maybe you've got too much fat up here," I said, tapping his forehead. "C'mon, maybe Mom and Dad are out in the garage!"

We raced through the kitchen and out the sliding glass door to the garage.

The windows were still blacked out. I

didn't even care. Whatever was going on, I had to talk to my parents! I had to make them understand.

"You know, if they are taken over by aliens and junk, maybe we should get some professional help or something," Roger suggested. "We could go on one of those talk shows."

I could see the show topic now: "Zombie Family Created by Killer Toilet." I'd look all sad and cry, and the host would hand me a tissue...all the kids at school would watch and feel so sorry for me that they'd give me their lunch money for years...

But I was getting carried away.

"We don't have time to get help," I told Roger. I started pounding on the garage. "Mom! Dad! Open up! It's me, Joe! Joseph! Joey! Whatever you want to call me is fine, just come out!"

"Don't get hysterical, dude," Roger said.

Then there was the sound of something moving inside, sort of scraping against the cement floor.

"Uh...I think I hear my mother calling me," Roger said nervously. He started to inch away from me.

I grabbed him by the shoulder. "You can't

leave me now, you dumb coward."

Then the door swung open.

It was my mom dressed in her welding suit!

She snapped up her visor and gave us this really creepy smile.

"Would you like a snack?" she asked. She was holding a fancy tray of weird-looking appetizers, including crackers with huge nut-covered cheese balls in the middle.

"I definitely hear my mom calling me," Roger said.

I took another look at my alien-esque Mom and said nervously. "Yeah, I think she's calling me, too!"

We both turned to run—and bumped smack into my dad!

He must have snuck around behind us while we weren't looking. He had on a welding suit, too. "Hello, boys!" he greeted us.

"H-hi, Dad," I stuttered. If he even *was* my dad anymore.

"Hello, Mr. Kohler," Roger said.

"Would you like to see what we've been working on in the garage all this time?" he asked us.

I shrugged. "Not really. You know me— never the nosy type! Listen, if you don't mind, I think I'm going to live with Roger and his family from now on!" Roger and I backed away from my folks the whole time I was talking.

"Oh, come on in, boys, take a look!" Dad said. "Pretty soon the whole world is going to know what we're doing in here—and we don't want you to be left out!"

He started herding us into the garage. We had no choice—Mom was on one side of us and Dad was on the other. We were trapped.

I looked at Roger and he looked back at me. Together we stepped into the garage.

It was absolutely freezing inside! And dark, too, like they didn't want anyone to know what was going on.

Which was true, I guess.

"Well, what do you think?" Dad asked.

I couldn't believe my eyes. Standing there in the middle of the garage was—

"A giant toilet, Dad?" I asked.

"It's not a toilet," Mom said, sounding offended.

"It sure looks like one," Roger said.

"It's a sanitary unit, boys. Don't be vulgar," Mom scolded us.

Vulgar? My parents have been secretly working on a giant toilet and we're vulgar?

It was huge—it went all the way up to the ceiling of the garage! There was a bowl, a tank, and up on one side, surrounded by a bunch of buttons and levers, was a giant metal handle!

It was so shiny, I could see our reflections. *Cynthia!* I thought. She must have been in here cleaning!

Only now she looked like a total mess.

Nothing was making any sense!

You totally lose perspective when you're staring at a two-story toilet.

Wait a second, I thought. Two stories! Just like the car-RV-toilet thing in Floville! "What—what's it for Dad?" I asked, almost afraid to hear the answer.

Mom and Dad looked at each other. Dad took a cracker off the tray Mom was holding. "Well, that's still kind of a secret, Joe, but I can give you a little hint." He picked up the softball-sized cheese ball and held it up in the air. "Imagine this is a planet," he said.

"Wow, that would be so cool!" Roger cried. "Like Mars, you mean?"

I punched him in the arm. "Shut up, cheese-*head*!"

"Listen up, you two. Say this cheese ball your mother made is a planet. A planet where there is a large population of creatures who are not particularly bright. Creatures that could be enslaved and destroyed with no great loss to the universe!"

"You mean...like Earth!" Roger cried.

Dad smiled. "Perhaps! Anyway, when that thing you think is a toilet is finally activated, here is what will happen to that planet!"

Dad's grip tightened on the cheese ball. His knuckles went white as he tried to crumble it into little pieces. He grunted and used both hands. It was pretty gross.

"Guess I should have used mozzarella instead of hard cheddar," my mom said.

"What would happen, Dad?" I asked him.

His face was getting red from smushing the cheese ball. Finally he threw it on the ground as hard as he could. It bounced slightly and started rolling away.

"Someone would throw the planet on the ground, Mr. Kohler?" Roger asked.

"No—no!" Dad cried. "It will be smashed into a thousand pieces—annihilated!" He picked up a hammer and started pounding the cheese ball, turning it into a flat orange pancake.

"But what's the point, Mr. Kohler?" Roger asked.

Dad's face was covered with sweat. He took a deep breath. "Maybe that was a bad example," he admitted.

"There's some French chocolate truffle mousse in the fridge," Mom offered.

Again with the gourmet chef thing!

Dad's face brightened. "Yes! Get the mousse, my darling! Then I will show you how a planet looks when it's destroyed and scattered on the solar winds!" he cried, raising his arms with joy. I was starting to think he should stop taking vacations.

"Four mousses then—I'll be right back!" Mom chirped happily.

"Did she say mousses or mouses?" Roger whispered to me.

"Hurry up!" Dad called after my mom.

Mom stopped dead in the garage doorway and turned back to Dad, frowning. "You listen to me, John Kohler! Just because we're helping aliens from another dimension invade and devastate the Earth is no reason to get snippy!"

"Invade the Earth!" Roger and I cried together.

Then a voice boomed out from the garage. "Enough of this foolishness! Prepare the Earth children for transport!" the shadow said.

"Yes, Supreme Commander," my parents responded together.

I couldn't believe it. The Supreme Commander of the aliens was—

CHAPTER
11

My sister? She'd always been bossy and organized, but this was ridiculous!

Cynthia stepped into the dim light, wearing ratty jeans, a black T-shirt, and a NEW YORK YANKEES baseball cap backward.

Cynthia?

I ran over to her. It couldn't be! My sister couldn't be the Supreme Commander of an alien invasion force! She didn't even drive a car yet!

"Cynthia, what's going on?" I demanded.

She looked at me and smiled. "Not much." She took a big drink out of a can she was holding. Then she held it out to me.

"Care for a drink?" she asked.

I stared at the can in horror. Beside me, Roger gasped.

"Darling Debbie Strawberries 'n' Cream Bath Bubbles!" he burst out.

"Yeah, it's really refreshing! It does a body good!" Cynthia announced.

"Bring them to me now!" she said in a scratchy, scary voice. A bubble popped out of her mouth and floated up to the roof.

Mom and Dad came up behind Roger and me.

"Where are we going?" I asked.

"We are going"—she paused dramatically—"to the bathroom!"

"No!" I screamed.

"You can't make us!" Roger yelled.

I looked at him, rolling my eyes. Like we'd be able to resist these freaks!

We were marched into the house. The walk up the stairs was the longest hike I've ever taken in my life. Everyone was completely silent.

When we got to the bathroom, Cynthia took the key to the lock out of her pocket and began to unlock the door. "Now this won't hurt you one bit," she said to me.

Where had I heard that before? Maybe before the doctor zapped my wart.

I turned to my mom. "Mom, if this has anything to do with not cleaning up the basement bathroom, I'm sorry! I was sick, remember? And I didn't have time and—"

"Silence!" Cynthia bellowed.

"What's going to happen to us?" Roger whimpered.

Cynthia smiled. "Oh, nothing much. Your brains will be melted down to mush and you will live out the rest of your miserable lives in a barren world."

"You mean...there's high school on this planet we're going to?" I asked.

"I'm going to be in big trouble if I'm not home in time for dinner," Roger told her.

"I wouldn't worry about that if I were you. Your parents will be joining you shortly," she informed him.

Then we heard the voice from downstairs.

"Hello, is anybody home?"

Aunt Thelma to the rescue!

Mom and Dad and Cynthia looked at one another.

This was our big chance to escape!

Grabbing Roger by the shoulder, I dodged between Mom and Dad and rushed down the stairs.

"We're here, Aunt Thelma, we're here!" I cried.

Roger and I were down in the living room before anybody knew what was happening.

Aunt Thelma was standing at the door. I ran up to her and practically mowed her down.

"Hey there, Joe–Joe," she said. "What's the matter, sweetie?"

Where do I begin? I thought. *With the weird bathroom or the giant toilet in the garage or the invasion of Earth? Or the fact that my sister was threatening to take me to another planet?*

But before I could say anything, another figure appeared in the doorway. I gulped. "It's him!"

CHAPTER 12

It was that toilet-shaped salesman from the Gleepnorp toilet store in Floville!

Was he Aunt Thelma's boyfriend, or what?

He held out his hand and smiled. "Hello there, young man," he said.

"Run, Roger! Out the side—go—go!" I yelled.

We made a dash for the sliding glass door. I could hear Aunt Thelma and my parents shouting as we ran across the yard.

Roger and I ran all the way to his house.

"So, what do we do now?" Roger asked once we were safely in his bedroom.

Roger's room was Armies of Evil Central. There were posters and Armies of Evil junk all over the place.

"I'm not going to any stupid alien planet, that's for sure!" I told him.

I was still in a state of shock. Our new toilet was an alien transporter. And my dad had built a giant one for mass transportation of earthlings back to some warped alien planet!

"You can't stay here forever," Roger said.

"Thanks a lot, dorkbreath," I said. "I wouldn't stay here even if you wanted me to You heard what Cynthia said—your parents are going to get flushed, too!"

"I hate your sister!" he cried.

"You didn't hate her last week!" I said.

Maybe the aliens would possess Roger next—I could only hope.

"Okay, maybe I had a crush on her," he admitted, "but now that she's the Supreme Commander of an alien invasion force, I think she's a sicko!"

"Me too," I agreed. "But she's still my sister. I have to save her if I can." I got up to leave.

"Where are you going?" Roger asked.

"To the bathroom," I told him.

"Okay, but don't mess it up like at your house. My mom would kill me," Roger said.

"Not *your* bathroom, doofus, *my* bathroom. I'm going back."

Roger gasped. "But didn't we just escape from there?"

"Exactly. So the last thing they'll expect is for us to go back, right?"

"I guess," Roger admitted. "I don't know about the *us* part, though." He got up and went over to his dresser.

"I don't expect you to come with me, dude," I said, feeling incredibly noble. "This is my family and my problem."

Roger pulled his official Armies of Evil Galactic Empire issue Kolodner 800 out of his drawer and belted it on his waist. "I'm going with you, dorkbrain," he said, drawing the Kolodner 800.

I got up and high-fived him. "All right! But what do you expect to do with that Kolodner 800?" I asked him.

He pointed to the INTENSITY dial on the side. "It makes six sounds, dude. Remember? Maybe we can use those freak-a-zoids."

We kept under cover all the way back to my house. Crouching behind Mr. Gumpitz's hedge, we surveyed our target.

"How are we going to get in?" Roger asked.

"We have to get up on the roof and go in

through the window," I told him.

"But what if they're all still in the bath-room?"

"That's a chance we'll have to take," I said, sounding a lot more confident than I felt.

I took a deep breath. "Okay. We have to get around the side of the porch and climb up on the roof. Ready?" I asked.

"Yeah," he said.

"All right—let's move out," I told him.

Suddenly, he grabbed me by the arm. "Hey, Joe, who's the king of Armies of Evil?"

I started to tell him that I was. But the geek was going to help me save my family, after all.

"You are, pinhead," I told him. "Let's go!"

Roger jumped up on the porch banister. I gave him a boost and he was on the roof in a second. He crouched down on the shingles and waved for me to join him. I climbed up on the banister, grabbed the edge of the roof, and started to pull myself up.

"Roger, give me a hand!" He grabbed me by my shirt and started to pull as my feet dangled in mid-air.

Then I heard the front door open. Someone was coming!

"Hurry, dude!" I cried. I squirmed and Roger pulled. I had just swung my legs up onto the roof when I heard my dad.

"Is somebody out here?" he called.

Roger and I didn't even breathe.

Suddenly Roger looked as if he was going to sneeze.

I clapped my hands over his whole face. My dad walked around awhile. Then we heard the door open and shut again.

I took my hands away from Roger's face. Then we stood up and inched our way toward the upstairs bathroom window. When we got there, I peeked inside.

Empty. Cool!

But the bathroom sure looked different...

"Let's go in," I said to Roger as I slid the window open. "I'll go first."

I pulled myself through the window. Roger was right behind me.

"Hey, what happened to this place?" he said.

The bathroom walls were covered with geometric drawings and weird writing that looked like a code of some kind. The room was absolutely freezing, just like the time when the toilet tried to chop off my head!

"What do you think this writing and junk

is?" I asked.

"Well, it isn't the recipe for a cheddar cheese ball, I'll tell you that!" Roger said.

I walked over to the toilet and felt around behind it. I found the secret panel almost immediately.

"What are you doing?" Roger asked.

I didn't answer him. Instead, I searched under the sink until I found the Darling Debbie Disinfectant Spray. Then I walked back over and started punching buttons and flicking levers behind the toilet.

"Hey, dude! Don't do that," Roger said. He pulled his Kolodner 800 out of his holster and aimed it at the toilet.

I kept punching buttons.

"Dude, what are you doing?" Roger demanded.

I stepped back and put my hand on the handle of the toilet—or alien transporter—or whatever it was. Then I turned to Roger.

"I'm going to flush. And something's going to happen. Either we're going in, or something's going to come out. Whatever is there, if it lives in the toilet, then it's a germ! And if it's a germ, it isn't going to like this one bit!" I held the disinfectant spray up and pointed it at the toilet.

"If we go in, we'll find the aliens and zap them out of our lives! You ready, man?" I asked.

Roger planted his feet firmly on the bathroom floor and gripped his Kolodner 800 expectantly. "Go for it," he said.

I put a little pressure on the handle—and flushed.

The water in the toilet started swirling up and out of the bowl, surrounding us and sucking us in!

"Aaahhhh!" Roger screamed.

CHAPTER
13

When I opened my eyes, Roger was lying beside me. I reached over and shook him a little. "Roger, wake up!"

He rolled over and said, "Oh, Mom, I had this awful dream." Then he opened his eyes. "W—what happened?" he asked.

"I don't know. But don't worry—Mommy's right here," I teased him.

"Oh, that's so funny I forgot to laugh!" he shot back at me.

"Thumb-wrestle to the death!" I cried.

We both stood up at the same time. That's when we found out that we were inside a toilet!

It looked exactly like the toilet thing that Dad had been working on in the garage except we weren't on Earth anymore. There were stairs leading down from the bowl. We climbed down them and looked around.

"It looks like a sewer," I said.

"Yeah, and it smells even worse—kind of like you," Roger said.

"Ha, ha," I said.

But I had to admire the stench. It was incredibly bad.

We were in a big round room with two hallways leading off in two directions. The floor was all slimy and yucky. The toilet thing was right in the middle of the room.

"That must be the transporter device for the invasion," I said.

I took a few steps away from it and something slimy ran over my foot. It looked like a snail with legs. It made this really "gooshy" sound as it slithered away.

"Hey, Roger! I think I just saw your long-lost twin brother," I said.

"No way, dude!" Roger said. "It's your brain—you better catch it!"

"Shh," I told Roger. "What's that?"

For a minute all we could hear was the steady *drip-drip* of the slime running down the walls. And then—there it was again!

It was just a whisper. But it was a whisper that I knew all too well.

"Come on!" I cried. "This way!" I started down one of the corridors leading off the transporter room.

Roger came running up behind me with his Kolodner 800. "Where are you going, dude?" he asked.

I pointed up the corridor. "Those voices were coming from the end."

"Yeah, but—" he started to whine, and then—*splat!*

He took a step toward me and fell backward into the slime. "Ewwwww!" he cried. Slime splashed up and a horrible rotten egg smell rose from the floor.

I reached out to pull him up. The slime made a sucking sound. I pulled harder and Roger tried to stand up. "Man, this is gross!" he cried. Finally there was a big *splootch*— and Roger was standing beside me again.

I looked at his back. "You are totally covered with super-disgustingness, man. Wait until we tell everyone at school how we trudged through an alien sewer."

Suddenly we heard a familiar voice at the other end of the corridor.

"Gleepnorp? Is that you? You let us out of here right this minute!" the voice demanded.

It was my dad!

I took off running with Roger right behind me. The slimy tunnel went on for about fifty more feet. Then we emerged into a bright room. There were huge control panels all over the walls, with millions of tiny buttons and lights. Surveillance screens were hanging from the ceiling, and giant joysticks, taller than me, were planted in the scum-covered cement floor.

I kept running toward the small, plastic bathtub-shaped bubble at the end of the control room.

My family was inside the bubble! They were all still dressed in the clothes they had worn that day in the bathroom before the toilet sucked them in. My dad was just wearing a towel. My mom and Cynthia both had their robes on and towels wrapped around their heads.

I ran over to them and yelled, "Mom, Dad, Cynthia!"

Dad started waving his arms and yelling at me. "No, Joe! Stop!" His breath fogged up the clear plastic.

I stopped and Roger ran into me from behind. What a dork! "Dad, Mom, what's going on? Where are we?" I asked.

My mom called out, "Joe—stop! There's a force field or something between us!"

"The control panel for the force field is on that console over there!" Dad pointed toward a bank of flashing lights to my left. "I think it's the third one down from the right—the flashing blue one!"

I went over and pushed the button. It stopped flashing. There was a kind of crackling sound. Then the walls of the plastic bubble completely dissolved!

My dad stepped toward me. Mom followed him and Cynthia came last. My sister looked really scared.

"How do we know these are really your folks?" Roger whispered to me.

I realized the dorkus was right. I *didn't* know. I wanted it to be my family. But if they weren't, who were they? And what had happened to my real family?

Then my dad said something that made my blood run cold. "I don't know how you got here, Joey, but I'm sure glad you did!"

Joey! That's what the other dad had been calling me for the past week!

Then his hand shot out and toward my head, and I knew I was a goner!

"No, don't!" I shouted.

"What's the matter, Joe?" he asked. I felt his hand grab my ear and tweak it a little.

The alien dad had never done that!

113

"Dad!" I cried. "It's really you!"

Dad frowned. "Who else would I be?"

Before I could say anything else, a laser sound blasted across the control room.

Roger had his Kolodner 800 leveled at my dad, and he was blasting away on STUN INTENSITY!

Good thing it was just a stupid toy gun!

"Cut it out, Rog," I said. "It's really them!"

Roger holstered his weapon. "Sorry, Mr. Kohler, but you can't be too careful!"

"Boy, am I glad to see you two dorks!" Cynthia said in her same old snobby voice.

"I should have left you in there," I said.

"Stop fighting, kids. We've got to get out of here!" Dad said. "I think I can operate the transporter in the other room!"

"But, Dad, what's happening? What's going on?" I demanded.

"Joe, we have to hurry. I'll explain everything when we get back!" he promised.

Suddenly, there was a huge slurping sound and a gurgling voice boomed, "I'll do all the explaining, if you don't mind!"

Cynthia screamed.

Mom fainted.

Roger turned green.

"Gleepnorp!" Dad cried.

CHAPTER
14

Gleepnorp? But Gleepnorp was supposed to be back at our house—with Aunt Thelma.

I turned around and saw why Cynthia was screaming. It was the same awful face I'd seen in the toilet!

It was a horrible puffy blob with bright red eyes and a really narrow mouth. The blob kind of blobbed forward a little. Suddenly a horrible stink hit us.

Roger nudged me in the ribs. "Man, I didn't know aliens stunk so bad!"

Suddenly, one of those slimy little snail things quivered across the floor in front of the alien. The alien's mouth opened, a bright yellow tongue shot out, and the snail disappeared down its throat.

"Gross!" Roger and I cried together.

"Care to join me for lunch?" the alien asked with an evil laugh.

"Gleepnorp!" my mom yelled. "I demand that you release us this instant!"

The blob just laughed some more.

"But, Dad, how can that be Gleepnorp?" I asked.

Before he could answer, the alien waddled forward again and stared at me. "How nice to have you here, Joe-Joe!" he said.

"Don't call me that, Gleep-Gleep!" I warned him.

"Oh, I am sorry. I forgot that you don't like that name! In any case, let me answer your question. I am Gleepnorp!"

I sneered at him.

Bad move. The alien looked pretty peeved. "I am Second Lieutenant in His Sliminess Chief Executive Officer Gragolg of Polaris's army!" he cried. "And I am forward scout for the invasion of the Earth! You are on my scout ship—ten billion miles from Earth!"

"You know what, dude?" I said. "If we're going to be on the same scout ship, then you're going to have to take a bath. You stink!"

I was doing my best Wolverine impersonation ever. It felt great!

"You'll get used to the smell," he assured me, his red eyes glinting. "You're going to be with us for a long, long time!"

"So who's the other Gleepnorp?" I asked.

"A simple matter of mind control, the first step in our invasion plan," Gleepnorp explained. "Perhaps it was a mistake to use my real name. But no matter—the plan is working perfectly!"

"Why were my android parents calling me Joey and treating me like I was a kid again?" I asked him.

"It appears that some of our information on you was outdated. We are ten billion miles from Earth, you know."

Just then we heard a *squish-squish-squish*, and two shadowy figures appeared in the doorway. They stepped forward—and the doorway slid closed behind them.

Roger and I gasped.

It was *us!*

"Just in time!" Gleepnorp announced. "I recently lost contact with the human you knew as Gleepnorp," he continued as the fake Roger and I moved toward us.

"But now with your family unit replaced with androids, and more and more mini-sanitary unit transporters being sold and installed in your puny world, there is no chance that our plan can fail! Once your father-replacement android finishes work on that mega-transporter, division after division of His Sliminess's storm troopers will be transported. Intelligence agents will appear in bathrooms everywhere, overwhelming your world from within and without! You are finished, Earthlings!"

What a dork! I thought. Like I hadn't figured out his stupid scheme when I was sucked down the toilet! I hadn't heard such a long speech since the Thumb bored us with that Shakespeare dude.

Suddenly, Roger stepped forward. "I don't think so, slimebrain!" he cried. He aimed his Kolodner 800 at the alien and fired. The gun made a laser-like sound.

Gleepnorp laughed. "A toy laser—how charming!"

Roger twisted the INTENSITY dial. A new kind of rapid-fire laser sound began.

"Stop! You're killing me!" Gleepnorp gasped.

I pulled the Darling Debbie Disinfectant Spray out of my back pocket.

"Hey, that's mine!" Cynthia cried. "Who said you could mess with my stuff?"

I wondered for a second if there was any way of "accidentally" leaving Cynthia with the aliens.

Gleepnorp looked at me. "What do you have there?" he asked. "Is it a present for your new leader? Hmm?"

"Yeah. It is for you, as a matter of fact," I said, holding the can behind my back. "But no fair peeking!"

"You will learn to respect me or you will suffer!" the alien cried, sliding toward me.

There was nothing standing between me and a slimy death!

I got ready to spray while Roger frantically twisted the INTENSITY dial on his Kolodner 800. Suddenly there was a beeping sound and a recorded voice boomed out of the gun.

"Congratulations, Galactic Warrior!" it announced. "You have enabled the Kolodner 800 Secret Option!"

Roger stared at the gun and then at me. The Kolodner 800 had started smoking!

Gleepnorp lunged toward it and the toy gun made a loud, long whistle. Gleepnorp started screaming and sliding all over the place.

"Turn it off! Turn it off, Earthling! I beg you! It is the death whistle of my people.

Turn it off!" he pleaded. Then he collapsed on the floor.

Roger and I gave each other a high-five.

"Cool!" we yelled at the same time.

"See, Mom?" I cried. "I told you all that time playing Armies of Evil wasn't a waste!"

We ran over to where Gleepnorp was writhing on the slimy floor. I pulled the disinfectant from behind my back and aimed it at his face.

"Meet Darling Debbie, germbrain," I said.

"Yeah, sewerbreath. Say hello to freshness!" Roger added.

I sprayed him as if he were a large bug. Gleepnorp started melting and getting all gooey as soon as the stuff hit him. Maybe there was something good about Darling Debbie after all. Maybe I could bring it to school and try it out on the Thumb. And I owed Lumpy, too.

"He's dead!" Cynthia cried.

"We're free!" my mom yelled.

"There's only one problem," I said.

"Should we bury him?" Roger asked.

"I'm not touching that thing!" Cynthia declared.

"No, it's Aunt Thelma!" I cried. "She's all

alone with the androids. Come on, we have to get back to the house!"

We all ran over to the toilet transporter.

I knew my dad would be able to work it. He's one of the best engineers in the world. Plus, he's been using toilets for years.

"Brace yourself, everybody!" he said.

We all held on to one other—and Dad pulled the handle!

We materialized in the upstairs bathroom. I tried to open the door. Then I remembered that the androids had locked it from the outside.

I took a step back and hurled myself at it, trying to smash it open.

"Ow!" I crumpled to the ground, holding my shoulder.

"Smooth move," Roger said.

"Yeah, ding-dong. The door opens in, not out!" Cynthia chimed in.

"What in the world have they done to our bathroom?" Mom asked. "Did you have anything to do with this, Joe?"

Dude, you save your family's life and what do you get for it?

"Mom, I busted my shoulder," I said.

"You shouldn't have run into the door," she told me matter-of-factly.

No sympathy at all.

I smiled. Good old Mom. I had my family back for sure!

"All my Darling Debbie stuff—it's ruined!" Cynthia cried. "Look—they left the caps off of everything!"

"Now, Cindy," Dad said. "We can replace your things. But first we have to get out of the bathroom!"

Then we heard a loud scream. It was Aunt Thelma!

"Stand back, everybody," Dad ordered. "I'm going to kick the door down!"

He kicked at the door. Nothing happened.

He kicked at it again and the doorknob bounced off. Aunt Thelma was screaming at the top of her lungs.

Dad kept kicking. "C'mon Roger, Joe—give me a hand!" he finally cried.

Roger and I started slamming the door with our feet. Dad pushed and tore at the wood.

"Just stand back, everybody," Cindy said. "Or we'll never get out of here!"

She crouched on the floor. "Give me a T. Give me an H. Give me an E-L-M-A!" Then she jumped up, kicking her legs out in front of her, and *wham!* The door went flying!

"Thelma!" Mom cried as we all rushed down the stairs.

"Cindy, you're, like, amazing," Roger gushed.

"Shut up, dweeb," she replied.

At the bottom of the stairs we all stopped. "Aunt—Aunt Thelma?" I sputtered.

She'd really gone over the edge this time!

CHAPTER
15

"Hello, family!" Aunt Thelma said happily, waving a machete at us.

There were body parts all around her! There was no blood, though—just wires and junk sticking out and little sparks and buzzing noises.

"Glad to see you all made it back in one piece!" Aunt Thelma said brightly.

"Thelma! What happened?" Mom asked.

Cynthia picked up the head of her android double. "That is *so* not my nose," she sniffed, tossing it over her shoulder.

"Well, first I got Mr. Thompson here unhooked from the Polaris mind control network." Aunt Thelma nodded toward the toilet salesman we had first met as Gleepnorp. He was standing at the other side of the room, also carrying a machete. He nodded and smiled.

"Then I rushed back to see what had happened with you folks," my aunt went on.

"But I thought you were one of them!" I told her. "I saw your bike back at the toilet store!"

"Sorry about that, Joe-Joe. When I finally convinced Mr. Thompson that I could help him, we took his car," she explained. "I guess a polluted world is better than no world at all!"

"But how did you know about all of this— the invasion of the world and the androids?" Dad asked.

Aunt Thelma smiled. "Why, I have a subscription to *Wacko Monthly*. Just last month they had an article on some people who believed in androids and mind control. Can you imagine anything this bizarre happening right here, in our town?"

My father cleared his throat. "Yes, er... thank you, Aunt Thelma. And thanks to Joe, for coming to save us."

I shrugged. "No big deal." But I could see getting a lot of mileage out of this in the weeks and years to come. I saw myself asking for a convertible, Dad saying no, and me saying, "Remember the time..."

Roger picked up the android Cynthia's leg. "Can I keep this?" he asked.

Cynthia grabbed it from him. "No way!"

"But, Aunt Thelma, you already knew, didn't you? That day at the toilet place. And nothing had even happened yet! How did you do that? Do you have ESP or something?"

Aunt Thelma smiled at me. "Your Aunt Thelma might be a wacko, Joe—but she's not stupid!"

After some really lousy snacks my mother made—burnt microwave popcorn, rotting peaches, and warm soda—we went upstairs and destroyed the toilet transporter in the bathroom.

Then we dismantled the mega-transporter in the garage, and Mom went into her office to do some studying. Dad started picking out ties for the upcoming work week.

Cynthia was on the phone the minute we got back to Earth, telling all her friends why she'd looked so horrible at school that week.

They didn't believe her. Would you?

After dinner I went over to Roger's house. As a reward for helping us, his parents had bought him the brand-new version of Armies of Evil.

On the way over, I ran into Lumpy Leudke and Donald Blauvelt. "What's with the dumb belt?" Lumpy sneered, pointing at the Kolodner 800 I had strapped around my waist.

"You know nothing, foolish Earthling," I calmly replied, walking right past him.

Before we started our Armies of Evil marathon, Roger suggested we make up a new rap. We plan to become famous one day, so we're always looking for fresh material.

"Okay, hit it!" Roger yelled. He put his hands around his mouth and started making background noise.

I picked up his desk lamp, pretending it was a microphone.

> "We're alien mashers!
> We're outer space smashers!
> Don't mess with us 'cause
> We can mess you up faster!
> You stink and you smell
> And it's not hard to tell
> If you invade the Earth
> Then the Earth is gonna
> Blast ya!"

"Let's go downstairs and get something to eat," I suggested when we were done taping ourselves. "My mom's back to being a lousy cook. Got any cheese curls?"

We started down the hall to the stairs. On the way, we passed the bathroom.

The door was open. I glanced in.

Roger's dad was fiddling around with something on the back of their toilet.

"Look what we got today," Mr. Douglas said, smiling. "Your father's right, Joe, the prices in Floville are simply amazing!"

He put his hand on the handle.

"Mr. Douglas, don't flush!" I yelled.

"Dad, stop!" Roger cried.

It was too late. The toilet took on a green neon glow. The water in the bowl started swirling around.

"Déjà vu, man," I muttered.

Roger stared at me. "Huh?"

"Instant replay!" I yelled.

We quickly unholstered our Kolodner 800's. I grabbed a can of Darling Debbie Bathroom Beautifier off the shelf.

"Dude, you've got to let me zap the next alien," I told Roger as we were sucked down into the toilet. "If you don't...noogie time!"

"Don't you get tired of shoving people

around?" Roger asked as we headed through the tunnel into another universe.

I tried to give him my most ultra-concerned look, as if I was really thinking it over. "Actually, no! Never!"

Hey, if a guy doesn't have principles, he might as well be an android.

Speaking of which...

I hope Aunt Thelma chopped up the right one of me!

There's one more

Gooflumps

Don't miss R. U. Slime's other masterpiece!

#4 ½
EAT CHEESE AND BARF!

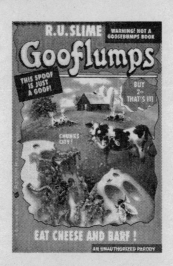

Another Unauthorized Parody
Not a Goosebumps Book